MARINE F: SBS

ROYAL TARGET

GW00357411

MARINE F: SBS

ROYAL TARGET

Robin James

For my good friend Dick Gobel, with many thanks for the computer crash course!

First published in Great Britain 1995
22 Books, Invicta House, Sir Thomas Longley Road,
Rochester, Kent

The name Robin James is a pen-name of James Hallums

The moral right of the author has been asserted

A CIP catalogue record for this book is available from the British Library

ISBN 1 898125 46 5

10 9 8 7 6 5 4 3 2

Typeset by Hewer Text Composition Services, Edinburgh
Printed in Great Britain by Cox and Wyman Limited, Reading

1

Something in the air was making the almost-invisible line of hairs on Leonard Dobbs's spine tingle. He had been in Her Majesty's Prison Service for far too many decades to be deceived by the overall aura of calm which had been pervading the atmosphere of his jail for more than a week. Prisons were not like that. It was very seldom that a day went by without a scuffle or argument of some sort, or a week without an ugly brawl. Yet recently there had been hardly a raised voice, never mind a threatening fist. It was unnerving. Parkhurst Prison, at Newport on the Isle of Wight, was hardly a finishing school for young ladies. It was one of Britain's toughest top-security prisons, housing some of the most violent of the country's convicted criminals, a bunch of men with their tempers generally on the shortest of fuses.

Dobbs had taken over as Governor of Parkhurst from J.R. Marriott only three months previously. He had been moved from London's Pentonville, another unlovely establishment housing dangerous men. During his five-year governorship there he had had murder and mayhem – and a bloody riot – to contend with. There had been frequent fights between inmates, and trouble between inmates and warders. Had he been required to describe the atmosphere he would have said it was one of constant unease. But never in all that time, or in his short period at Parkhurst, had he come across such a period of tranquillity. It was as if the entire prison had suddenly gone mellow from the effects of marijuana – which, given the fact that drugs and other undesirable commodities found their way inside the grim walls no matter how supposedly tight the security, was possible but hardly likely.

A basically kind man whose exterior had been toughened by his vocation, Dobbs had been pleased to be moved from London to the fresh air and comparatively relaxing environment of the Isle of Wight. He and his wife and three teenage daughters had been housed in a small, comfortable detached residence close to the sea and he was looking forward to the possibility of spending the final seven years of his working life there.

As he dropped his youngest daughter off at school on that overcast Wednesday morning in July 1995, the Governor of Parkhurst was a most preoccupied man, too concerned with a lingering premonition of imminent disaster to notice that the girl had left her satchel on the back seat of his

Rover until he had almost reached the forbidding walls of the prison. Good father and family man that he was, he took the trouble to take the satchel back to the school even though it made him late for work.

His tall, erect, trim, elegantly clad figure appeared somewhat out of place as he was let through the harsh outer doors of the jail by a warden whose uniform seemed to be in need of a good pressing. Leonard Dobbs looked more like a banker than a prison governor, and indeed there had been many times during his lengthy career when he had wondered why he had not chosen a profession such as that. Yet his personality fitted the job, for he was a man who could find a degree of compassion for almost any of his charges, however heinous their crime, and as such he ruled prisons well, always fighting the difficult, often near-impossible battle for reform.

Once in his office that morning, Dobbs spent an hour tending to his mail and phone calls, then made his customary tour of the prison accompanied by two guards. Again he encountered what seemed to be an unnatural calm. He had brief words with several of the inmates and they were polite to him as always, for he was a respected man. But in one or two of them, especially the mass murderer Ulrich Warren, he felt sure he detected a diffidence which was put on for his benefit, as if they were trying to hide something.

As the Governor left the carpentry room, a pair of eyes the palest of eggshell blue, eyes as cold and as hard as two diamonds, followed him out. The eyes were set in a swarthy, good-looking, fortyish face beneath a broad, wrinkled forehead suggesting keen intelligence. That face belonged to an international terrorist, Venezuelan-born Arsenio Cruz Conde, a man as infamous as Carlos the Jackal. Arsenio was known by the Spanish-speaking world as 'El Asesino' – the Assassin – and with great justification.

While he preferred a 'job' where advanced warning was to be given before a bombing, in order to spare the lives of the innocent, or one that involved the taking out of a person who – in his view – patently deserved such a fate, nevertheless Arsenio's powerful hands were stained with the blood of people who had inadvertently got in his way. Once committed to an act of terrorism he was merciless, and the fact that unnecessary deaths would later trouble a conscience which he would rather be without never stood in the way of his unholy thirst for money. He was a master of disguise, a man of many superbly contrived identities, an expert in several varieties of unarmed combat, and an authority on weapons and explosive devices with contacts worldwide to supply them wherever they might be needed.

The expertise and infamy of the Assassin had led to him being contacted by the IRA to take charge of their most audacious campaign since the

1985 Brighton bombing – and that had led to his downfall. It was the reason he had begun serving a triple life sentence in Parkhurst eight months previously.

As Arsenio watched the Governor's erect back disappear beyond the barred door of the carpentry room, and that door was locked by a warden, he ran his hands over the smooth soundbox of the Spanish guitar he had been lovingly and superbly fashioning for weeks. His mind took him back to that fateful night in September 1993 . . .

Early autumn had brought with it a chill which suggested a cold winter in store. At nine-thirty in the evening, as the brightly coloured houseboat was slipped off its moorings by Kevin O'Leary, a crisp wind blowing south through the streets of Chelsea brought a tingle to the Irishman's busy fingertips. The boat, a converted barge whose fussy exterior decoration was evocative of an old-fashioned Romany caravan and whose interior was a warm and friendly blend of furnishings antique and modern, soft, pastel textiles and low, atmospheric lighting, was the property and home of thirty-year-old Rodney Mack and his wife Cynthia, the owners of a trendy interior-décor shop in Pont Street, SW1.

As the houseboat, which in a moment of supreme optimism Rodney had christened *Odyssey*, drifted out into the murky waters of the Thames, Mr and

Mrs Mack, attired in the evening clothes they had been wearing when about to depart for a charity dinner at seven o'clock, were lying, thoroughly trussed hand and foot, and gagged with a pair of Cynthia's mauve silk stockings, on their huge, specially designed bed, which fitted into the prow of the boat.

Arsenio Cruz Conde's assault upon the Macks had been carried out with adroit precision; the first the couple had known of the fact that there was an intruder on the deck was when the main hatch had been opened and a stun grenade had been lobbed down between them. When, none the worse for the attack, several seconds later they had recovered consciousness it was to find themselves being tied up by two burly men while a third was unpacking heavy metal tubes from a large wooden crate on the Persian rug in their stateroom. Cold fingers of fear clawed at the bellies of the good couple Mack as, realizing but not comprehending their plight, they saw that their assailants were wearing stockings over their heads; as his black-silk-socked ankles were secured with a nylon cord which bit into his flesh hard enough to cut off the blood circulation, Rodney began to tremble in terror. When, moments later, he was dumped, together with his wife, on the connubial bed his trembling made the mattress shake. Cynthia was so frightened that she peed herself.

The IRA powers that be had been unhappy with

the 1990 mortar attack on 10 Downing Street. It had been ineffective and all but bungled, the main reason being that the missiles and launchers were not up to their task. Having, early in 1993, dreamed up their most audacious assault ever, they determined that this time there was going to be no error, that they would employ modern assault weapons of deadly fire-power and accuracy – and a man who could both deliver the weapons and efficiently employ them. For that reason, Arsenio the Assassin was at the wheel of the *Odyssey* as she drifted eastwards with the strong currents on that late-September evening. He had been employed by the IRA to mastermind the organization, overseeing and execution of a plan so breathtaking that they could not trust any of their own operatives – skilful and daring though they might be – to take charge of it. Instead, harbouring no resentment, the most accomplished pair of the IRA killer squad, Kevin O'Leary and Tim Shannon, were under the command of Arsenio – and were awed by and proud of the fact.

In its conversion from a barge, the houseboat had been fitted with a small bridge in open plan with the stateroom itself. Wide, polished-pine steps led up into the bridge just before the door to the sleeping quarters. This was one of the reasons, during his covert but meticulous inspection of all the houseboats moored along the Chelsea Embankment and at Cheyne Walk, that Arsenio had picked the *Odyssey*. Another was that with her wide, flat bottom she would remain stable at the crucial moment, and recoil would not make her roll too heavily. A third was her bright and slightly eccentric appearance. Cruising down the Thames on a Saturday evening with lively music drifting from her – already, as they reached Battersea Power Station, Chris Barber's jazz band was raucously playing *Muskrat Ramble* on a CD which Arsenio had brought aboard – she appeared anything but sinister, the very antithesis of suspicious.

The trip was to be a short one; two more bridges to go under – Vauxhall and Lambeth – and they would be at their target. The bright lights of Saturday-night London twinkled on both sides of the river.

Arsenio switched on the engine. He had no need for it while they were drifting with the swift current, but shortly it would have to be put in reverse thrust – and then full speed ahead. He felt little tension at such moments as this, when action was imminent. He was possessed of a calm which was one of the most important secrets of his success. Where other men would be doing battle with their nerves, El Asesino would have every ounce of concentration on the job in hand, his acute intelligence analysing and reanalysing, looking for the tiniest flaw, the slightest deviation from plan which could cause disaster. It was for this reason that the man had never made a mistake and why he was always several steps ahead of the world's anti-terrorist squads. The nerves, curiously, came afterwards, when he was well clear of the scene of action. It was then that he needed comfort in the arms of a woman. Lately, she had been a vivacious little redhead, a secretary called Kirsty in whose anonymous little flat off the Cromwell Road he had installed himself and who understood him to be an advertising executive of Argentinian origin whose name was Alberto.

'Take over the wheel, Kevin,' said Arsenio. His voice was soft, yet commanded attention, the accent almost undetectable.

''Tis a fine night for fireworks,' commented O'Leary, mounting the steps. The Venezuelan turned an icy, cynical eye on him. The Irishman was clearly tense – jocular remarks on the brink of action were always a dead giveaway.

Arsenio grunted and replied, 'Hold her steady in the middle of the river.'

The Irishman's heavy hands – clad, as were Arsenio's, in fine surgical gloves – took over the wheel as the houseboat slid under Vauxhall Bridge; Barber's trumpet was bouncing through the final bars of *Muskrat Ramble*. The Tate Gallery, colourfully illuminated, was approaching on the port side. Traffic in Millbank was heavy, a slowly moving sea of light.

In the stateroom of the *Odyssey*, Tim Shannon had slid wide open one of the picture windows. On his knees on the Persian rug, behind a dull-metal M72 anti-armour rocket launcher with its block of four rocket tubes, he was carefully lining up the deadly weapon to the angle which Arsenio had most carefully worked out during several trips on hired boats on this stretch of the Thames.

'Load the son of a bitch,' Arsenio told Shannon. His voice was oddly flat, his eyes icy. The chilly north wind was blowing straight into the boat, ruffling his black, wavy hair.

'Four up the spout,' muttered the IRA man, as he lifted a 66mm anti-armour rocket from its wooden case and slipped it carefully into the launcher. 'Quads it is then.'

Arsenio studied Shannon as he slid the rockets one by one into their tubes. Nervous. You as well as Kevin, he thought. No wonder you make balls-ups. It's you that's almost having babies. He nearly voiced the thought, but decided against it.

The *Odyssey*, the steady chug of her engine being blown away south to Lambeth Palace Road as she passed under Lambeth Bridge, began to slow when Arsenio ordered O'Leary to put the engine in reverse thrust. By the time they drew level with their target, she would come almost to a stop. She presented a pretty sight, there in the middle of the river with all her lights blazing and the lilting jazz of *Canal Street Blues* drifting from her; many a motorist waylaid by traffic lights admired the brightly coloured angel of death.

But not only were people in cars watching the *Odyssey*. For security on this stretch of the river was tight – far tighter than Arsenio had discovered, or even imagined. In his trips he had taken note of the security cameras affixed to the ancient brown walls which housed his target. He was well aware that the crucial moment of action would be observed and recorded, but that fact did not bother him. It would be all over in seconds and they would have escaped into the night before any pursuit would be possible. But he had not spotted the almost-hidden cameras on the undersides of both Lambeth and Westminster Bridges – cameras pointing towards each other and thoroughly covering that critical three hundred yards or so of river. Most important fact of all, there was no way of knowing that the scruffy-looking, wooden boat shed below St Thomas's Hospital on the Albert Embankment housed an armed launch of the Special Boat Service – the SBS, the unit of the Royal Marines specializing in reconnaissance and sabotage.

It had been decided only five months previously – in the light of intense IRA activity – that the army, rather than the river police, should be in charge of surveillance of this important stretch of the Thames. Doubly dangerous for Cruz Conde's operation was the fact that this very evening was the time that Zaki Fernandez had picked for an inspection. This meant that the crew of patrol boat

11

Dart were on full alert, with two frogmen in full gear on stand-by.

Zaki Fernandez was of Greek and Spanish parentage, but had been born and raised in England as a British national. He was a formidable, experienced fighting machine who had gone right through the ranks of the army from corporal in the Light Infantry to captain of the Royal Marines and had lately been promoted to SBS major, a position in which he was much respected – and to a certain extent feared. He was six foot three and broad with it, a massive hunk of early-middle-aged manhood who by far preferred action to inspection, but such was his lot this evening.

The single pair of eyes which watched the two TV screens to which were relayed the pictures from the bridge-attached security cameras were widely spaced, chestnut-brown, intelligent. But for the presence of Major Fernandez on the *Dart* they might have been bored. For in Sergeant Stride's book this was – as it was for everyone else – a tedious turn of duty. Nothing ever happened, and the likelihood of action was slight. They had been called out once to assist in a rescue when a pleasure boat with a party on board had been sliced in two by a barge, and another time to apprehend a boat loaded with cocaine. But the possibility of such incidents was not the reason for their constant vigilance. Rather it was the historic building, the hub of the nation, which lay directly across the Thames from them: the Houses of Parliament.

Sergeant Stride watched the progress of the *Odyssey* as, slowing down and keeping to the centre of the river, she approached the western edge of the Houses of Parliament. Snatches of jazz, flung on gusts of breeze, began to meet his ears and he imagined, rightly, that they came from the brightly coloured houseboat. Well, bully for them. No doubt they were drinking, dancing maybe, canoodling, having a great time while he, dry, was obliged to sit here half the night in front of these effing TV screens. Such was the extent of the sergeant's thoughts about the houseboat. El Asesino had been absolutely right in his calculations – stick it right under their noses and they would see it all right, but suspect it they would not. He had failed, however, to realize the strength of the opposition.

Arsenio was on his knees on the Persian rug, making last-second adjustments to the aiming of the rocket launcher. The House of Lords was coming into view through the window. From within, here and there was a hint of light, but in effect the Lords was closed; there would be very few people inside on this Saturday night, for its business finished for three days each week from Thursday evening. The IRA wanted it more or less empty, for tonight's attack was to be a warning. Hit it a severe blow, show their muscle power. Next time

– very soon unless certain of their demands were met – they would hit the House of Lords again, sending 66mm anti-armour rockets hurtling through the high, stained-glass windows of the main chamber when the House was in session. And this time the rockets would not simply have high-explosive warheads – they would be loaded with napalm.

The prospect of many of the country's most distinguished elderly gentlemen and ladies being burnt to death while fire, threatening to consume the entire Houses of Parliament, raged all around them, would surely be so terrifying that the Government would at last give in to the IRA. Such was the plan.

'Slow her right down,' Arsenio called out over Max Collie's spirited rendition of *When You're Smiling*. As she came level with the House of Lords, the *Odyssey* was barely moving. In the police launch, Stride vaguely wondered why but it failed to alarm him. In any case, it was far too late to do anything even if it had.

Arsenio had set the M72 to fire a ripple of all four rockets. His finger was on the switch. Perfectly calmly, the hint of a smile on his lips, he moved to one side of the launcher and flicked the switch.

The noise within the houseboat was deafening. *Whoom, whoom, whoom, whoom* went the rockets as, close on one another's heels, they shot from their tubes on their perfectly aimed trajectories. Such was the recoil that Arsenio, even though he was prepared for it, was flung backwards into a bulkhead as the flat-bottomed boat was tipped to an angle of almost forty-five degrees and skidded sideways through the water. Both the Irishmen were thrown over, and in the prow the trussed Macks were crushed together between the curved edge of the bed and the side of the boat's nose.

'The whole world smiles with you,' warbled Max Collie gaily, as the rockets smashed their way one after the other, precisely through the windows of their target – the peers' guest room and bar.

'Go, go, *go*,' shouted Arsenio as he picked himself up. Oblivious of the fact that his head had cracked so heavily into the edge of a shelf in the wheelhouse that his temple was pouring blood, O'Leary slammed the throttle on full, and the *Odyssey*, still lurching violently from side to side in the wash caused by the M72's recoil, shot forward towards Westminster Bridge. Shannon, meanwhile, hurried around to kill all the lights and the music.

For a split second, Stride thought he was hallucinating. Then, as four powerful explosions followed the four heavy 'whump' sounds which had drowned out the jazz, and a section of the House of Lords erupted with smoke and fire, he pressed his panic button.

There was little need for the alarm. Fernandez's keen, highly experienced ears had recognized the first sounds for what they were and was hollering to the bridge to get the patrol boat out into the river even as the rockets smashed into the Lords.

The *Dart*, in its sleepy black hole of a boat shed, came alive in seven seconds. Within twenty, as the blacked-out *Odyssey* sped under Westminster Bridge, it was roaring out into the Thames, siren blaring, searchlights illuminating the water for one hundred and fifty yards in front of it as brightly as sunshine, and sending up a great wash of water against the walls of the Albert Embankment.

Arsenio's master plan had been to take the houseboat around the right-hand bend in the river at Waterloo Bridge, then under Blackfriars Bridge, and to abandon it at Riverside Walk, where it met Bankside, just before Southwark Bridge – where he had a driver and a fast car waiting for them. He had worked this out precisely as taking, including reaching the car, six and a half minutes. He would be away before London even began to realize what had happened. But he had reckoned without the presence and lightning reaction of the SBS.

When Arsenio heard the siren, and looked back into the blinding searchlights, he assumed that an armed river police boat was bearing down on them. He did not panic. Knowing it was folly, without the right fire-power, to do battle with the river police – he and the IRA men were not even carrying guns, and the remains of their only four rockets were white-hot, smouldering metal in the wrecked peers' guest room – he left the other two men to their own devices and hurried on to the deck to slither flat on his belly between the small bridge and the edge of the deck. His only chance of escape was to slip unseen into the water and swim for the south bank, staying as far beneath the surface as his lungs would allow. At a place where he had a chance of protection from eyes on the fast-overhauling launch – but where he risked, if he failed to drop like a stone, being hit by the propeller – he rolled over the edge close to the prow of the boat to hang for moments with his feet trailing in the wash. As he hyperventilated to enable himself to stay for the maximum time beneath the surface, he was staring directly through a porthole at the bed, from where his two trussed prisoners gazed out at him with wide and fearful eyes.

Steeling himself for possible mortal pain, Arsenio let go. He was lucky. As the chilly, mucky water closed over him he was bashed by the keel and spun around, but the propeller missed his head by inches. Cold already beginning to eat into him, and heavy clothing – he was wearing jeans, trainers and a thick roll-neck sweater – weighing him down, he struck out with a powerful breast-stroke to where he imagined the shore lay.

The slight inward curve of the prow of the boat had not been sufficient to disguise Arsenio's taking leave of it from Zaki Fernandez's sharp eyes. On the bridge of the patrol boat as it began to draw alongside the *Odyssey*, his gaze sweeping the surface of the water in the area where he had watched Arsenio disappear, the major ordered his armed frogmen to the rail.

Disoriented by his spinning around as he went under, Arsenio had been swimming in the wrong direction. When he came up for air he was almost beneath the SBS boat – and staring up at them as the frogmen went over the side after him. He had not the slightest chance, and he was far too intelligent to take one. Instead of diving beneath the Thames once again, he meekly raised his hands and surrendered. He even managed a shake of his head and a rueful grin.

Unhappily for O'Leary – and for Cynthia Mack – the Irishman was foolish enough to disregard Fernandez's loudhailer command to heave to. O'Leary began weaving the houseboat to and fro across the Thames, and a trigger-happy SBS sergeant manning a prow-mounted Browning M1919 machine-gun stitched the bridge with bullets, shredding him. Both of the boats were bouncing around in the water. The *Odyssey*, with O'Leary's bloody corpse hanging over the wheel, was out of control and heading straight for the Victoria Tower Gardens at Millbank. The *Dart* lurched by its side. A final burst of bullets from its machine-gun pierced the prow of the houseboat. The trussed and gagged Mrs Mack died instantly, her heart and lungs ripped apart.

The *Odyssey*'s nose crumpled into the river bank,

badly injuring Rodney Mack. The only people to have come out of the affair unscathed were Arsenio Cruz Conde and Shannon, both of whom would in due course receive triple life sentences.

To Arsenio's regret, the peers' guest room and bar had not been empty during the attack on the House of Lords. Two cleaning ladies had been working there at the time. It had taken a great deal of surgical skill and ingenuity to fit their appropriate pieces back together again for burial.

All that had been twenty-two months ago. El Asesino had been detained by these English whoresons for far too long. Apart from anything else, he was a man with an enormous sex drive, and the variety of sex readily available in Parkhurst was utterly repugnant to him. As he stroked the soundbox of his almost-finished guitar he mused that, if all went well, this would be his last hour inside HMP Parkhurst. Tonight, with luck, he would be in the arms of a woman and, *hombre*, was he going to show her what a South American *macho* was made of! But, he realized, he was going to miss his guitar.

In that moment he decided that even if it complicated his escape he was going to take his cherished creation with him.

2

Leonard Dobbs's uneasiness increased as the morning wore on. Yet he couldn't put his finger on
anything. His murderers, extortionists, rapists, con
men, thieves and terrorists had metamorphosed
into a bunch of model prisoners. It was utterly
unreal. In his office, just before lunchtime, he
studied the bank of security screens which shared
one wall with a colour picture of Her Majesty the
Queen, a framed map of the Isle of Wight and a
sprinkling of anodyne seascapes.

Men were beginning to file back to their cells
from workrooms, the gymnasium, library and
exercise yard, to wash for lunch. They moved in
orderly fashion, chatting quietly. And yet . . .

The Governor watched as Arsenio Cruz Conde
walked beneath the security camera on his way out
of the carpentry room. Here was an enigma indeed:
one of the world's most wanted terrorists before his
capture, so dangerous that he was known as the
Assassin, a man for whom three countries had put
in requests for extradition – no chance of it being

20

granted, of course, for a bomber of the House of Lords – but whose behaviour ever since setting foot in Parkhurst had been exemplary. Cruz Conde was that cliché, the model prisoner. So much so that he was allowed to take his guitar – as beautiful a piece of craftsmanship as Dobbs had ever set eyes on – to his cell with him to work on between carpentry sessions. Most carpentry tools were, since they could be used as dangerous weapons, forbidden beyond the woodwork room. But Arsenio had his sandpaper and his varnishes and his glue and some small vices in his cell, and his guitar took shape there almost as much as it was progressing in the workroom.

Something inside Dobbs's head was niggling at him to sweep the entire prison, to turn over every cell and workroom, to search for weapons. To discover why everyone was acting as perfectly as Cruz Conde always did – for surely there had to be a reason. On the other hand that operation had been carried out only two weeks before and to do it so quickly again would seem awfully fussy, if not downright provocative.

There was a sharp rap on his office door. He responded with his customary 'please', turning away from the TV screens as his head warder came in.

'Were you observing anything in particular, sir?' asked the overweight but thoroughly capable Officer Briggs.

'Browsing, if you like, John. Just browsing,' Dobbs told him as he went to his desk and sat down. He was sorely tempted to take a cigarette from the inlaid wooden box on his desk and light up. It was seven weeks since he had given up and the craving only seemed to get worse. With great control he put the idea from his mind – he had, after all, promised his wife and daughters that this time he was giving up for good. 'What's up?' he asked.

Briggs nodded at the screens. Prisoners were going into their cells, whose doors would not now be locked on them since they were about to go down for lunch. 'Something, if I'm not mistaken, sir. Just what do you see on those screens?'

Dobbs's deep-brown eyes, slightly troubled, flickered from his officer to the screens and back again. 'I see . . . serenity.'

'Too bloody much serenity by far. Am I right?'

'You too then?'

Resting his closed, hefty fists on the Governor's desk, Briggs told him, 'I've been in the prison service as long as you, sir. With respect, I believe I share your nose for it. Trouble's brewing. Something damned serious if you ask me. I had an idea you might be smelling it as well.'

'I do, John. I do. Very much so. I thought it was perhaps my imagination. But you've confirmed it isn't. Your recommendation?'

'That they have lunch. And afterwards we lock

them in their cells, we question everybody closely, we search everywhere with a fine-tooth comb, and we don't let them out until we get to the bottom of this bloody unnatural peace.'

The Governor produced a weak grin. 'Yes. Do that, John, will you. I begin to feel better already.' He straightened some papers on his desk and then sat back in his chair, deep in thought.

In the cell which he shared with the mass murderer Ulrich Warren, as the taciturn Warren was washing his hands, El Asesino, his back to the open, barred door, was stooping over his guitar, which was propped on its base on the single chair. Very carefully, he was prising off the hourglass-shaped back with the edge of a laminated playing card. The soundbox was so skilfully fashioned that its back fitted into the lipped sides with the precision of a bullet into the chamber of a gun, needing no glue to hold it temporarily in place. Even in this vital moment of his overall escape plan, Arsenio displayed his ironic sense of humour; for, as his tool to loosen the back, he had deliberately chosen the card of death – the Ace of Spades.

Very few people were capable of having a gun smuggled into a high-security prison, for the feat required the cooperation of expert outside help and was to all intents and purposes impossible without the subornation of a warder. It was probably unheard of for anyone to ever have got in two — and even less likely that he could have kept them hidden during a thorough search of the prison. The Venezuelan had achieved such a miracle.

Inside Arsenio's beloved guitar, taped to the removable back, was a Colt 1911 A1 automatic pistol and a tiny .20-calibre Russian PSM, whose bullets were powerful enough to penetrate body armour. Their clips were fully loaded, and there was a spare clip for each gun. The Colt he slipped to Warren, who tucked it away inside a makeshift shoulder holster fashioned from a strip of bandage, beneath his loose, brown-denim prison shirt. Then Arsenio pulled a thick elastic band over his shoe and up under his trouser leg to above his calf and jammed the PSM inside it. Two convicted assassins were fully prepared for a lively lunchtime in Parkhurst Prison.

Although the scene appeared relaxed enough, there was an air of tense expectancy in the lunch hall as the inmates queued for their meal and took their trays to their tables — which fact bothered Officer Briggs even more than the week of protracted calm. He thought that he could sense trouble in the air, but there was little he could do simply on a hunch. Besides, after this lunch everyone was going to be locked up until he had sorted out whatever it was that was going on. He warned the three supervising warders to stay very much on their toes.

As he placed his tin tray on the table before him and took his seat, Arsenio had a crystal-clear picture in his mind of how the next twenty minutes were going to proceed. He was perfectly calm and relaxed, utterly confident of success. He waited until everyone was seated and eating, then he called out loudly for a warder, an offended tone in his voice.

The warder had no reason to be wary of the Venezuelan, for Arsenio was one of the most popular prisoners – clearly there was something very amiss with his food.

'Look at that,' Arsenio complained indignantly, as the warder reached his side. 'Will you look at that, man. A fucking great black beetle in my cabbage. Christ.'

At that moment Dobbs happened to be staring at the screen in his office which covered the lunch hall. Though there was no sound, he realized, as the warder stooped to stare at Arsenio's food, that the prisoner was registering a complaint. At the same moment he observed something else as well – and it made his spine creep. So far as he could make out, every one of the prisoners had stopped eating and all were paying close attention to what was happening, although amid what should have been a general hum of chatter none of them except those closest to the terrorist should even have noticed. He hurriedly reached for his in-house phone.

There was a beetle all right. A broken-legged but

still living creature which Arsenio had produced from his pocket to stow among his cabbage. The warder picked up a spoon and poked the insect as Arsenio, apparently scratching his leg, slipped the PSM from its elastic band and swept it upwards to jam it painfully just below the man's right ear.

It was the signal for action, the moment they had all been waiting for. El Asesino had not only bribed a warder in order to get his guns into the prison, but had also offered a sum of money to most of the inmates – to be delivered to their families – in exchange for their participation in a riot as cover for his and Warren's escape. The money was hardly a fortune – £500 when they accepted, and the same amount when Arsenio was free – but it was enough, as he had expected, to encourage these long-term prisoners into the sort of activity which a great many of them would relish.

The other two warders were drawing their guns. As Arsenio shouted to them to drop their weapons or he would shoot their colleague, Warren dragged the Colt from under his shirt and unnecessarily put a bullet in one of them. The man sank to the floor, blood spouting from his femoral artery.

As the Governor stared at the dining-room monitor in horror, although not entirely in disbelief, the scene before his eyes transformed from the unnatural tranquillity of the previous week or so to one of utter mayhem. Every man was on his feet, tables were being overturned, plates and

26

knives and forks were flying, chairs were being smashed. Warren held the second warder with an arm wrenched behind his back and the muzzle of the Colt rammed into the man's neck, and had forced him to the locked and barred door, where he was threatening the guard behind it with death to his colleague if the door was not opened.

Dobbs watched his screen for several frozen moments. Then he punched his Grade One Emergency button and, with barely a thought for his safety, rushed out of his office. By the time he reached a viewpoint on a catwalk, men were spewing out of the opened dining-room and through the main hall towards the doors to the exercise yard, several of them now with warders' guns in their hands and firing indiscriminately into the air. Detached from them, coming up the stairs towards Dobbs, was Arsenio, his eyes calm and with even a hint of amusement in them, the crook of his arm around Briggs's neck, his PSM in the back of the man's head as he forced him forward.

'This is total madness,' the Governor called out, realizing as he shouted them the futility of his words. 'You'll never get away with it.'

Arsenio stopped a short way from him. 'Get back into your office and call the guards off the walls,' he told him.

'I can't do that.'

The Venezuelan was not a man to waste words. He put a bullet through Briggs's forearm. As the

27

man screamed in pain, Arsenio said flatly, 'Next time it's his cock, all right? Unman the guard posts, Mr Dobbs.'

'The police, the army, they're already on their way. You haven't a chance. Nobody will even get out of here, never mind off the island.'

'So call off the guards. Or maybe you want to see this one a eunuch and the rest mangled – or dead?'

Dobbs sighed heavily. Illusions, when they died – and they frequently did in this business – died hard. He had been utterly convinced that in Cruz Conde he had a reformed character on his hands, a man who one day in the distant future, paroled, might make a decent contribution to society.

'I'll call off the guards,' he said.

In his cell, Arsenio allowed Briggs to clumsily bandage his left hand, which was streaming blood, then he tied both of the warder's hands behind his back with a strip of linen previously torn from a bed sheet for that purpose. He had used another strip to fashion a makeshift strap for his guitar. Slinging the guitar over his back, he ordered Briggs to walk in front of his pistol. They started off down into the madness raging below them.

In the exercise yard, the most violent of the prisoners had gone further than was necessary – or than Arsenio wanted them to. Perhaps what had sparked off these excesses was Warren's shooting of the warder, who would now be bleeding to death but for the intervention of a convict who had had compassion enough to staunch the flow of blood by applying a tourniquet around the man's upper thigh. The prisoners had captured nine warders, stripped them naked, and were ribaldly taunting and humiliating them.

Well, fuck them – they could sing for their other five hundred quid, thought Arsenio. And if Ulrich Warren was labouring under the illusion that his cell mate was going to take a dangerously unstable mass murderer out of Parkhurst with him, then he would not be for much longer.

Knowing what was about to happen next, the rioting prisoners cleared a path for Arsenio. Once amid the safety of their numbers he released Briggs, and he was now being followed by Warren into the centre of the yard, where Tim Shannon, also serving a triple life sentence for his part in the House of Lords rocket attack, was waiting for them.

The helicopter was already descending, a thin, flexible ladder, seventy feet of it, hanging below it and bouncing and jerking with the chopper's vibrations. The small, company-owned, four-seater Dragonfly had been hijacked – although with the paid collusion of one of the staff of a private flying club near Southampton – just fifteen minutes earlier. The hijacker was a completely dependable terrorist colleague of Arsenio who was used to split-second timing, a one-time militant right-hand man of Dr George Habash, the leader of the

Popular Front for the Liberation of Palestine. Libyan-trained in his mid-teens, thirty-eight-year-old Palestinian-born Joseph Hantash was all round as useful as Arsenio himself – piloting a helicopter being but one of his many skills – as ruthless and as interested in making making money with his prowess as El Asesino, now that the Palestinian cause was gradually being peacefully resolved by Yasser Arafat.

The Dragonfly reached an altitude of sixty-eight feet, more than twice the height of the prison walls, where it hovered noisily. Arsenio nodded at Shannon, who began running up the ladder with the agility of a monkey climbing a palm tree. He was already inside the chopper by the time Arsenio grabbed the ladder and put one foot on its bottom rung.

Dobbs meanwhile, greatly perturbed by this new development, and realizing now why Cruz Conde had forced him to call the armed guards off their towers, appeared on the small balcony of his office overlooking the exercise yard, and raised a powerful megaphone to his mouth. His echoing words filled the yard, louder even than the motor of the chopper and the swish of its blades.

As Arsenio made his way up the ladder, wind from the rotors tearing at his hair, Warren, preparing to start an ascent behind him, with one hand on the ladder, raised the muzzle of his Colt 1911 A1 and lined up its sights on Dobbs. He then proceeded to carry out an action so grossly unjust and unnecessary that Arsenio would have done anything in his power to stop it – he squeezed the trigger and succeeded in putting a bullet clean through the megaphone, through Dobbs's face and out through the back of his head. Dying, the Governor of Parkhurst tumbled over his balcony and crashed down two floors into the yard.

The sound of the shot made Arsenio glance sharply down and around, quickly enough to see Dobbs hit the ground. He was, in any case, about to yank up the ladder and have the chopper lift off while he was still climbing, stranding Warren. Now he was so overcome with rage at the man's action – he had, like any intelligent prisoner, entertained enormous respect for the Governor – that he carefully aimed his baby .20-calibre PSM and drilled a neat hole through the top of the murderer's skull. Then he made the agreed sign to Hantash and, as he continued to climb the ladder, clinging perilously and swaying in the wind, the helicopter soared high above the prison.

Below them, fast shrinking until they were no larger than toys, police cars, army vehicles, ambulances and fire engines were converging on Parkhurst Prison. Reaching the open door of the helicopter, Arsenio hauled himself inside. He was feeling bad about Leonard Dobbs. He was of course going to be held responsible – and the killing of Ulrich Warren, while in his view completely justified, was yet another murder on his record sheet. Every move he made, for the rest of his life, was going to have to be with the greatest care and planning. Well, he reflected, it was going to be like that anyway. Indeed, it had been for many years. Sliding into the seat next to Hantash, he greeted him with a curt nod.

'Hey, man,' said the Palestinian. 'How's it going?'

'Tough. But at least the buses around here are dead on time.' Arsenio lit a Camel and inhaled deeply.

'I don't like that word.'

'What word?'

'Dead.'

El Asesino grunted. He glanced at the altimeter: twelve hundred feet, levelling out. There was no point in climbing higher – they would be a blip on a police radar screen by now and would in any case be descending shortly.

'What did you bring a guitar for?' asked Hantash, glancing at the instrument. 'It's got no strings on. It isn't even finished.'

'Sure, and didn't you know he's a soft, sentimental creature, so he is,' grunted Shannon, in the back.

'I'm going to finish it.'

Arsenio looked down. They were crossing the choppy waters of the Solent, with ahead of them the sprawling port of Portsmouth. Another minute and the city was passing beneath them, to its north the verdant landscape of Hampshire. He knew better than to ask the Palestinian if everything was in place; he had never known the man – who had no record or irritating notoriety as he had himself – to screw up.

Ten minutes later the Dragonfly was making its descent. It landed in a remote part of the South Downs, close to a narrow road on which was parked an unassuming, slightly dented Ford Escort. They had not seen anybody during the landing and transfer to the car, but just in case they were observed and the number-plate was noted, Hantash had another vehicle waiting in a small village south of Horsham.

A mere forty-five minutes after discovering a black beetle in his cabbage at Parkhurst, Arsenio Cruz Conde, El Asesino, and Tim Shannon, the IRA killer, were being driven at moderate speed towards London in a stolen Mercedes 380SL with changed number-plates to match the immaculately forged papers.

3

Kirsty Childs had created the perfect setting for a candlelit dinner. In her neat little flat in Lexham Gardens, just around the corner from the Cromwell Road, she had laid the table for two, with an Irish linen cloth, stylish sterling silverware and two tall, thin, tapering red candles in silver holders, to match the elegantly coned napkins. An open bottle of respectable claret stood between two gleaming, cut-crystal glasses, and the smell of roast tenderloin of beef wafted from the cottage-style kitchenette to share the air with the cool sounds of John Coltrane's tenor sax. Kirsty's latest boyfriend was about to arrive on the scene and she was happily buzzing around her flat puffing up cushions, her thick, dark hair glinting copper in the candlelight, her firm breasts trembling beneath a frilly, white cotton blouse which accentuated her considerable cleavage.

Kirsty was a stunner, a curvaceous twenty-eight-year-old who turned heads wherever she went. Five feet six and a half in her stockinged feet, when dressed in one of her impressive collection of high-fashion outfits she looked every inch a model or film star. But she was neither. To her friends, family and boyfriends she was secretary to a newspaper executive – a position about which she was reluctant to make more than the most superficial of comments; for the job was a lie of three years' standing.

Kirsty Childs was a con artist, and a very good one. Bored with life in a lawyer's office, disillusioned with the pay – and with men in general, for she had been unable to form a stable relationship since the love of her life walked out on her when she was twenty-two – at the age of twenty-five she had turned to a financially reward-ing life of crime. Kirsty knew much about that subject, since her office specialized in defending criminals, and, gutsy and strictly speaking amoral rather than immoral, she had tackled her new life with great professionalism and success. Credit-card fraud was her main speciality, though she had also developed – learning from her experience in the lawyer's office – various ingenious little systems for cheating banks out of cash. She had had a couple of narrow squeaks, but she had never been caught, partly because she confided in absolutely no one and worked strictly alone. Her entire wardrobe, worth many thousands of pounds, had been obtained with stolen or forged credit cards, as had the silver and glassware which adorned her table. Kirsty was more pleased with herself than she had ever been in her life on the straight and narrow, though to describe her as totally happy and contented would be an exaggeration, for there had been one, comparatively recent, major event in her life which had deeply saddened her.

The doorbell rang. Well, here *he* was, waiting outside in the slight drizzle which had just begun, for her to let him in via the entryphone. She had high hopes of this one. Her most recent of conquests showed all the possibility of actually being a real man, and not turning out to be a complete wimp like so many before him. She had had so many bad experiences with the male sex that at times she almost wished she were a lezzie. But this one was an excellent performer in the sexual department, a stayer in the sack, unselfish. And above all he was strong and self-confident, not afraid to tell her, in the nicest possible way, what he expected of her in both behaviour and dress. But even as she let him in the communal door and opened the front door of her flat to receive him, she reflected that no one was ever going to completely take the place of the one she still pined for, that charismatic man who, like her, almost two years ago had turned out to be living a lie which made hers seem like the most harmless of childish fibs.

They had got as far as a passionate embrace and kiss, after which she had closed the door and gone into the kitchenette and he was pouring himself a Grant's Scotch over crackling rocks, when the telephone rang.

Kirsty's face, as she listened to the voice of the man on the line – a sound she had thought she would never hear again in her life – underwent a dramatic transformation. It was at first amazed, then puzzled, then her cute little nose wrinkled in delight and her deep sea-green, widely spaced eyes began to sparkle.

'I'll be there,' she said.

The new boyfriend's annoyed protests were treated with stoniness. She was sorry, she had to go out, she had to leave right away, their evening was cancelled. Even as she told the stunned man that, she was pulling on a thin sweater. She turned off the roast, blew out the candles and, full of excitement, took her lover down to Cromwell Road, where she hailed a cab and left him standing in the drizzle under a street lamp, watching the cab with a disgruntled, angry expression on his face as it bore her away towards Soho.

Arsenio Cruz Conde had been sitting in a café across the road from the Three Feathers public house on the corner of Old Compton Street and Charing Cross Road since calling Kirsty from the pub. In the window, he had been attentively studying the face and bearing of everyone who entered the pub to see if they bore any possible resemblance to a police officer. For although El Asesino felt reasonably confident that Kirsty would not betray him – she had not come forward at the time of his arrest for the House of Lords rocket bombing although it had been widely publicized, with his picture, which she must have recognized, splashed over every newspaper and TV news programme – he could not be certain of that fact and was not about to take the slightest chance.

By the time, a mere fifteen minutes after his call, she ducked out of a taxi and hurried through the thickening drizzle into the pub, only half a dozen people had entered the café and not one of them appeared remotely like a policeman. Nevertheless, he was still not satisfied.

Arsenio crossed the road and entered the Three Feathers, standing just inside, a lock of black hair plastered to his forehead by the rain, until Kirsty spotted him – which was in a matter of seconds because her eyes were darting all over the pub. She recognized him immediately, despite the heavy beard and moustache and the tinted glasses. Nerves all keyed up, heart thumping, she approached him, but, as he had told her on the telephone, without making any outward sign of recognition.

Before she reached the one great love of her life, the man whom she had never been able to put out of her mind despite knowing that he was a dangerous terrorist, he jerked his head at her – without any change in his flat expression – in a gesture that she was to follow him, and hurried out into the rain. He did not go far. He walked quickly down Old Compton Street, turned left into Dean Street, crossed Shaftesbury Avenue and slipped into the Duke of Wellington pub in Gerrard Street. During this short journey he stopped three times to watch Kirsty until she had almost caught him up, making absolutely sure she was not being followed. She, meanwhile, acted exactly according to his instructions, betraying no sign of recognition of him.

At the bar of the busy pub he finally smiled at her, took her into his arms and kissed her on the lips.

'You still drink Scotch?' were his first words.

'On occasions such as this I drink triple Scotches,' she said, '. . . in rapid succession.'

So he ordered three triple White Horses, on the rocks, and a bottle of soda. They took them to an empty table. Even now, he was cautious; he chose a table close to one door from where he had a clear view of the other.

'I'm not absolutely sure I like the beard,' she told him, studying him. 'It makes you look older.'

He took a long sip at his whisky, smiling at her. *Por Dios*, she was lovely, every bit as much so as he remembered her. 'Neither do I,' he said. 'It's false.' He squeezed her soft, pampered, light-fingered hand. 'If you like, I'll take it off.' He gazed deep into her eyes. 'Later, when we are alone.'

Her heart skipped a beat. Alone. She squeezed her thighs together. 'Yes.'

'You must have known I got out? It must have been on the news?'

'I haven't heard the news or read a paper since yesterday. It was today then?'

'Yes.'

'From Parkhurst? Were you still in Parkhurst?' She emptied one glass. It burned her throat and made her splutter, but she desperately needed it; she was a bundle of nerves.

'Yes.'

'I didn't think anybody ever got out of Parkhurst.'

'I did.' He paused, a hand on her designer jean-clad knee. 'You never tried to get in touch with me. Neither during the trial nor after it.'

'Nor you me.'

'I didn't want to involve you. Girlfriend of the man who rocket-bombed the House of Lords. Not good for you.'

'The same went for me. I didn't want to be involved. I loved you, but I was scared.' She sipped from her second glass. The contents of the first were already doing a good job of calming her nerves.

'And now?'

'And now what?'

'Are you still in love with me?'

'I think so, yes,' she said slowly. But she did not really need to consider her answer. She loved him without question.

The nostrils of his handsomely aquiline, almost aristocratic nose flared. His hand slipped up her thigh. How he needed a woman. Any woman to his taste would have done at that moment. Had he been unable to contact her he would have picked one up, or bought one by now and already been relieving his almost two-year-old need. But here she was, his lovely Kirsty, and now that the business of making sure she had not betrayed him was over, the scent of her, the touch of her, her beauty, was beginning to overwhelm him. He was getting the beginnings of an erection just from being close to her in this rather seedy, smoky pub.

'Do you still have the same flat?' he asked her.

'Didn't you just ring me?'

'People sometimes move and take their numbers with them.' He swallowed some Scotch, watching her closely. A lumpy knot of excitement had formed somewhere in the region of his lower throat and upper chest, refusing to budge – not that he wanted it to.

'Are you living alone?' he asked.

'Yes.' And thank God for that, she thought. It was going to be difficult enough getting shot of the present boyfriend, never mind a live-in one.

He finished his drink and got to his feet. He was about to pull her up when he remembered something. 'The police – they never questioned you? Never associated me with you?'

'Why should they have done? *My* you was an Argentinian advertising executive called Alberto, remember? And none of the stuff you left in my flat told me anything otherwise – and, believe me, I hunted through it item by item. I was waiting for them to put some heat on me, but it never happened.'

He chucked her pointy little chin. 'Some heat? Where did a nice girl like you pick up street language like that from?'

'I worked in a criminal lawyer's office for years, remember?'

His sexual need was getting more pressing by the second. If he didn't get her home shortly, he would be making love to her in the cab. He tugged her hand. 'Let's go, Kirsty.'

Butterflies swarmed in her belly as she stood up. 'Let's go, yes.'

She had blown out the candles and turned off the oven, but in her rush of nerves Kirsty had forgotten to switch off the CD player. It was on shuffle, and as she turned on a light and closed the door, Charlie Parker was playing the slow, sexy *Lover Man*. The number could not have been more appropriate – though love was not exactly the name for what both of them had on their minds at the explosive moment when they fell into one another's arms. Raw, uninhibited, raunchy sex was a much more fitting description.

Without breaking a kiss which had their tongues mingling and slithering against each other like writhing serpents, he ripped open her Moschino belt. She let loose a little squeal as she then found herself spun around in his arms and shoved to the dining table, though she made no effort to resist as he dragged down her jeans zipper and bent her over a sturdy, cane-backed chair. She gasped as his smooth but tough, artistic hands – which could be so gentle when making love – grabbed the sides of her jeans and rucked them over her hips and down her thighs. Her white silk Dior knickers followed. Kirsty's hands, with their perfectly manicured, mauve-nailed fingers, were flattened on the table top, the thumb of one touching the base of a silver cruet, the other hooked around a heavy candlestick.

Arsenio grunted as he opened his own zipper and impatiently fumbled down his trousers and underpants far enough to free his genitals. His penis was a large, solid, desperately needful animal craving for release. As with one hand he guided it in her, he slid the other beneath the loose edge of her blouse, under the lacy bottom of her skimpy bra, and grabbed her breast with a savagery born of almost two years' abstinence.

His roughness echoed the frantic need which had grown within her. Though she squealed as he groped and twisted her breast it was not from the slight pain he was causing her; it was a lustful pleasure noise. She had been damp between her legs ever since, in the pub, she was filled with the urge to make love to him. Her vagina greeted his manhood with a welcoming contraction, then he plunged all the way into her until his testicles were crushed between the upper backs of her thighs.

It was crude and it carried with it the hint of violence, this home-coming coupling, this hungry man going at his horny woman like a dog at a bitch on heat – and it was not destined to last for more than the shortest space of time. Arsenio was banging it in and out of Kirsty so hard that the chair was rocking and the table was shaking. Her auburn tresses were dancing around on either side of a silver platter, and he could see the reflection of her wide eyes and her gleaming little, white teeth behind her slack, drooling mouth before, as orgasm rushed upon her, she screwed her lids shut.

There was no way Arsenio could have held himself back, even had he wanted to. Twenty-two months' need for a woman had built inside him a mountainous frustration. Seconds later, as Kirsty raised her head and howled at a corniced corner of her room, all that frustration flooded from his testicles and into her with his semen as his hips slammed into her bottom so powerfully that the open bottle of wine and both the candles crashed over.

They stayed, panting, sweaty, locked together like that, unmoving for long moments until their heartbeats began to settle down. Then, hands on her buttocks, watching his action, savouring it, he slowly withdrew his wilting penis from her.

'Wow,' she groaned, as she slowly straightened

up from the table. 'Oh, *wow*.' She brushed her hair back from her face. Her jeans fell below her knees to concertina on her shins.

Arsenio was zipping himself away. His gaze drifting to her pussy as she turned around and pulled up her knickers, he said, 'Sorry to take you like that. To be so quick.' He shrugged. 'It just had to be, you see?'

She gaped at him. A lightning screw it might have been, but it had been extraordinarily fulfilling, the most incredible she could remember since the last occasion with this most attractive man – the prowess of her latest lover notwithstanding. She felt utterly drained, positively satiated. Her knees had gone weak and wobbly.

'*Sorry?*' she echoed as she lethargically reached for her jeans. 'Has being banged up turned your brain? Christ, it was great. It was marvellous.'

He grinned lazily. 'I'm glad. *Hola*, Kirsty.'

'*Hola* – what was it – El Asesino?'

He didn't take that so lightly. 'It wasn't how I was christened. I am unhappily stuck with it for life.'

She buckled her belt. 'Have you killed many people?'

'Please don't ask.'

'All right. Sorry.' She remembered how there had been two cleaning women in the House of Lords on that infamous night and that they had been rocketed to pieces. She had told herself at the time that it must have been an accident, that he could not have possibly known about them. She decided it might be prudent not to comment on this. She recalled the roast. It was still less than an hour since it had been ready, so it would warm up nicely. Moving to him, she snuggled into his arms. 'Hungry?' she asked him.

'I will be again, very soon. Then I'm going to take you to bed and fuck you long and slowly.'

She sighed, and planted a warm kiss on his lips. 'You better had. But right now I'm talking about hungry for food.'

'The table was set for two. Who was he?'

'Was, is all you need to know.'

'Right.'

'How would you like some roast beef?'

'Have you any idea what I've had to endure in the way of food these past two years?'

'You'd like some roast beef.' She broke away from his arms. Her eye fell on the table. There was half a bottle of expensive claret over the cloth, a huge red stain. 'Why don't you change the tablecloth, open a fresh bottle of wine and light the candles? You know where everything is. I'll fix dinner in a trice.'

A little later, as they tucked into the beef, Arsenio asked Kirsty, 'What did you think when you discovered I was a terrorist?'

'It was an incredible shock. I thought I was going to go out of my mind. I didn't know what to do

– but then there was nothing I could do. I waited for some sign from you. When there was none, and I realized I was probably never going to see you again, I was deeply, deeply sad. I can't begin to tell you how much.'

'I imagined you were going to be very angry. Indignant that I had been lying to you for those few months, living a double life. Shattered to discover that I was a wanted terrorist.'

'But I was in love with you, Alberto. Arsenio. Of course, in the light . . . I reassessed my feelings. They had got more complicated, but they didn't go away. I couldn't stop loving you no matter how much I wanted to.'

'Stick to Alberto. I'm your Alberto.'

Thoughtfully, she washed down some beef and roast potato with wine, studying him as he ate. 'That's how it was, Alberto. That's how it is.'

As they were finishing, he asked her, 'So how is the job?'

She carefully laid her knife and fork together on the plate. She said to them, 'There was no job, darling,' then raised her eyes to his.

'What do you mean, there was no job? Of course there was a job. You were a secretary.'

'I was a secretary, yes, once – to a lawyer. But I gave that up long before I met you.'

'Yes. And you were a secretary in some other company or other.'

She finished her wine. The coming confession

was perhaps going to be more difficult than she had imagined. 'Like you, my darling,' she said, slowly, 'I was not exactly as white as the driven snow.'

He shook his head at her, totally puzzled. He lit a cigarette, a habit he had acquired in Parkhurst and one which he was determined to give up. She did not smoke. 'I don't understand you, Kirsty. I mean, you went out to work every day. Promptly at eight-thirty in the morning, you left. You always kissed me and told me you loved me.'

'And? So did you go out. You were always dressed when I left, finishing your coffee. Where *did* you go, by the way?'

'Here and there. Meetings. Planning things. I had an anonymous little flat in Soho Square where I stow away my many identities. I still have it. I have another in Barcelona, under a different name. The police never broke me. The anti-terrorist police have never found out more about me than my real name and nationality. I am Arsenio Cruz Conde, and I am Venezuelan.'

'I know. I read everything that ever appeared about you.' She frowned. 'It's going to be difficult to stop calling you Alberto.'

'That is one thing I don't want you to do. You must not get into the habit of calling me Arsenio.'

'No. I do see why.'

He put out his cigarette. She was beginning to clear away the plates, musing as she did this about

48

exactly how she was going to tell him her dark secret. As he watched her, a fresh heat began to invade his loins. He got up, went to her in the kitchenette, where she was putting the plates in hot water, and took her by an upper arm as his other arm encircled her waist and he reached up to fondle her breasts – no impatient, greedy, mangling grab this time, but a gentle caress.

'What we two are going to do right now,' he said quietly into her ear, 'is we are going into your bedroom, we are going to undress one another until we are quite naked, we are going to make love for an hour – or maybe two – and afterwards you will explain your little mystery to me.'

The telephone was ringing. She ignored it. It was almost certainly him. A tight little knot formed deep in her belly. Her loins twitched. She flattened her hand over the crutch of his trousers, gratified to discover a hardening bulge there.

'You want to get into my knickers again? So soon?' she asked wickedly, her voice sexily throaty, her hand squeezing.

'It's been at least half an hour.'

The next five minutes were in no way as controlled as he had anticipated. In her bedroom, fires of passion again raged. In their craving for each other's bodies they almost tore each other's clothes off. But once he was inside her they settled down.

They did not make love for two hours, but it was

not far short. Afterwards, lying naked by Kirsty's side, flat on his back, watching a ceiling which, French style, she had papered with a tiny flower print to match the walls, he asked her what she had meant by not having been going to work.

When she finished telling him he digested the information – which had perhaps been one of the biggest surprises of his life – for a long time. Then he chuckled. The chuckle turned into a guffaw, and then roars of laughter. Tears came to his eyes.

She frowned. 'It's not *so* bloody funny,' she told him.

His laughter calmed down. 'Oh, but it is, it certainly is,' he spluttered through it. 'It's hilarious. Me being so very cautious not to make the slightest slip in front of you, you carefully hiding your real life from me. Both of us a picture of respectability. Both of us villains without the other having the slightest clue.'

'I'm not a villain,' she protested.

'Tell that to the jury.'

It was her turn to laugh. Then she said, 'So you see, I had more than one reason for not getting in touch with you after your arrest. I could hardly afford having the police coming around here, asking me lots of questions, turning the place upside down. They'd find all my special gear, my credit cards. Christ, almost everything I own is stolen one way or the other. I . . .'

He was laughing again, loudly enough to shut her up. Through it, a word at a time, he got out, 'We seem to be the perfect couple. The perfect bloody couple.'

4

Everything had gone as smoothly – and as anonymously – as she had desperately hoped it would. In her convertible Mercedes she had driven her close friend, Carolyn Parker-Reed – a tall, slim, attractive blonde bearing so striking a resemblance to herself they might have been sisters – and the children to Stansted Airport, where a Lear jet belonging to American billionaire industrialist Travers Bonnington had been fuelled and was waiting to whisk them down to Llanera, an airport south of Gijón, in the north of Spain. From there it had been a short hop in his private helicopter to Bonnington's 210-foot luxury cruiser the *Mirabelle*, moored in the calm waters of a bay off Salinas, some twenty-five kilometres west of Gijón.

There could hardly have been a more ideal hideaway for a princess constantly hounded by paparazzi, and who was arguably the most sought-after magazine subject in the world. The summer weather was ideal: bright-blue skies and a gentle breeze to take the bite out of the sun. The sea, a dazzling blue, was clear and cool, and they were so far from anywhere that it seemed perfectly safe to take a tender into the small harbour at Salinas with the kids – Diana nevertheless heavily disguised in dark, granny glasses and wearing a short black wig – to dine now and again on the excellent local seafood in a small bar-restaurant.

She had been there for five days, having a most restful time, developing a tan, swimming often, enjoying the delightful company of her backgammon fanatic of a host – he had once got through to the semi-finals in the world championship at Las Vegas – and his bubbly young wife, and making full use of the extensive leisure facilities of the *Mirabelle* – the games room, the gymnasium, the ski boat, the jet ski.

The Princess of Wales was beginning to feel perfectly unwound and – for her, a rare eventuality – utterly contented.

However, somehow – for they possess a legendary collective nose akin to that of a pack of foxhounds – some Spanish paparazzi had got wind of her presence.

It was just before lunch. There had been a rising wind. To the north, the Bay of Biscay was beginning to cut up rough, but in their bay it was still only a little choppy. Diana and Carolyn Parker-Reed – the eldest daughter of the Home Secretary – the two boys with them, had been taking it in turns to man the wheel of the speedboat, and to water-ski. Carolyn was driving, and Diana, topless, was skiing when the princess noticed that a small speedboat with what looked like four men in swimwear was approaching them fast. It was rare for there to be any other boats apart from fishing boats in the area, but as far as Diana was concerned when she first spotted it, it was no more than an irritation. Then, as it closed in, she saw the dreaded evidence of the profession of those on board: the black snouts of huge telephoto lenses pointed in her direction.

Frantic, Diana yelled and waved her arms, signalling to Carolyn to stop the boat. She sank down into the protective water, slipping off her skis. Only her head, and the floating skis, were above the surface as Carolyn closed in to pick her up. She managed to put on her bikini top, which Carolyn handed to her, before scrambling into the boat – but she did not secure it properly and as she hauled herself over the side it was torn off.

The paparazzi were by now almost alongside, and brief, enormously valuable shots of the royal breasts were taken before Diana had again clipped on her top. She was furious. The language she flung at the photographers as, ceaselessly shooting pictures, they followed the ski boat back to the *Mirabelle*, could not by any stretch of the imagination have been described as royal.

Aboard the billionaire's yacht, there was a brief, urgent conference as the rat-pack continued to circle. Observing the paparazzi from the French period-furnished stateroom as a second small boat came out to meet them, he saw something changing hands. The second speedboat immediately turned around and headed back towards the harbour. Travers Bonnington commented, 'That'll be the rolls of film, Diana. I'm afraid they'll go jet service to Madrid and be on offer to the highest bidder by this time tomorrow.'

Diana sighed. On her face was a mixture of sadness, resign – and anger. 'I was having such a super time,' she said. 'I didn't think the bastards would ever catch up with me out here. Why for Christ's sake don't they leave me in peace?'

'It's not going to be the end of it, either, darling,' said Carolyn. 'They'll be swarming all over us before we know it.' She forced a wry little smile. 'My tits should be so sought after!'

Despite her concern, Diana managed a giggle.

'I'm not going to give them the chance,' Bonnington said. 'We're getting out of here now before your British scruffs fly in. Guarantee they'll be here within a couple of hours or so and this quiet little bit of sea's going to look like a Disneyworld lake on a Sunday afternoon.'

The waves in the bay were steadily getting higher and longer, rolling in to sweep the golden beach. The paparazzi's boat was dipping and pitching in the swell, but they were still shooting pictures. Bonnington got through to the bridge on the internal line and ordered the captain to weigh anchor and head north-west. Twenty minutes later, the *Mirabelle* was cutting its way through steadily roughening sea, the photographers' speedboat being buffeted on all sides as it followed. Ten minutes after that, as the *Mirabelle*, hardly disturbed by the sea apart from a gentle rolling, reached a comfortable cruising speed of twenty-two knots, the speedboat, tossed around like a cork and in danger of being swamped and sinking, gave up the chase. It turned around and began to head cautiously back towards Salinas, the paparazzi unconcerned about the soaking they were getting since, despite giving up the chase, they had secured pictures worth perhaps half a million pounds.

The Princess of Wales could, of course, have opted to take the helicopter back to Llanera and from there the Lear home to England – and she was offered this facility by her ever-attentive host. But she preferred the alternative. Her days on the yacht had turned out to be sublime; she did not yet want to face again the harsh realities of her tough world.

Bonnington was delighted to continue to accommodate her in any way she wished. After a discussion with Diana and Carolyn Parker-Reed, during which the three of them pored over a nautical map, it was decided to head for an area of sea around the north-west corner of Spain, some twenty-one nautical miles off the city of La Coruña. The weather forecast for the following day was a return to calm seas and a continuation of the sunny, warm conditions. The *Mirabelle* could ride at anchor with only fishing boats coming anywhere near them there, and Diana and sons and her friend Carolyn could sunbathe, water-ski and swim to their hearts' content until either the sea cut up rough again or they got thoroughly bored with it all.

El Asesino much preferred Barcelona to London. His hardened soul was in any case basically Hispanic, and he could live in the Catalonian city in the Spanish fashion, which meant warm, civilised nights where one could dine and drink – outside on terraces, if preferred – until far into the night, with a wonderful choice of first-class restaurants and selection of food and in an atmosphere far removed from the unemotional tawdriness of London.

Barcelona by day was a splendidly elegant city, with its wide, sweeping boulevards, many or which allowed a clear view from one side of the city to the other, its glorious parks and open spaces, its historic buildings – especially those designed, like the famous church of La Sagrada Familia, by Antonio Gaudí – its museums and art galleries, its throb and its bustle. The climate, too, was splendid, especially through spring and summer and into autumn, when it remained agreeably warm.

That was not to say that Arsenio did not have a soft spot for London. He enjoyed it for its theatres and cinemas, its great variety of architecture, its frequent elegance, its pubs, its multi-cultural society in which he could disappear like a shadow in the shade, its parks and wide open spaces, and its brashness and cynicism.

Arsenio had spent a great deal of time in other cities of the world. He would elect to be anywhere that was not enclosed by prison walls, but given the choice he would be in either London or Barcelona – and if he were obliged to pick one or the other it would be Barcelona.

It was eight days after his spectacular break-out. He never had fulfilled his promise to Kirsty in the Duke of Wellington to remove his false beard and moustache. It was too much trouble to replace and it was crucial that he be heavily disguised at a time when he was being looked for all over Europe. Kirsty did not much like it – but it was her macho lover Alberto hiding behind it and that was the only thing which really mattered. By now a good, thick stubble had pushed its way through beneath it and he could risk getting rid of it.

Arsenio's hidey-hole in Barcelona was smallish, like that in Soho Square, unassuming, and owned by him in the name of Alberto Mondini, for whom – as he did in several other identities, including the one who controlled his numbered Swiss bank account – he possessed a full set of false but perfectly documented identity papers, including a driving licence. To maintain each flat he had a local bank account in which he never had less than enough funds to cover three years' overhead expenses – such as local taxes – and all costs, including that of a cleaner, were covered by standing orders. Whenever he moved from either of his two flats he always took the precaution of telling neighbours and the cleaner that he expected to be away for an extended period, perhaps more than a year, thus covering the eventuality of a sojourn like that at Parkhurst without raising suspicion in anyone's mind.

He had telephoned his cleaning lady before leaving London, and he and Kirsty had walked into a flat perfectly aired and smelling of the three dozen freshly picked roses the woman had bought on his instructions. Kirsty found the place agreeable enough, though its situation, in the area of Las Ramblas, was akin in atmosphere to how Soho had been in the sixties. It had been cleaned up by the police for the 1992 Olympic Games so as not to tarnish Barcelona's image to the world, but now the area had returned to its old self with a vengeance as a centre of sex clubs, pornography, prostitutes and transvestites, thieves and con artists – a sleazy vitality which Arsenio happened to like having outside his front door.

The flat was in a slightly run-down turn-of-the-century building possessing a tawdry sort of elegance. Arsenio's flat on the third floor over-looked the regular pitch of rent boys and the same overweight whore – now even more overweight than ever – who had patrolled that part of the central, traffic-free, kilometre-long stretch of bars, bookstalls and stands selling anything from exotic birds to esoteric sex aids the last time he had been in residence almost two and a half years before.

Arsenio and Kirsty were having a tough time getting rid of his false beard, but it was gradually coming away. It was not the cheap theatrical variety hanging by hooks from his ears; it had been stuck on, as had the moustache, clump by clump, and getting it off, especially now that there was a real growth of whiskers beneath it, was a painstaking and painful process. They had been at it for half an hour, Kirsty applying frequent fingers of solvent, Arsenio, not trusting her, tugging away and ouching like a baby.

'You've been very closed-mouth about why we're here,' she was saying. 'Can't you tell me now?'

He shrugged, then grimaced as another clump of hair came away from his chin. 'Truth is, I don't know,' he said, dropping the hair into a waste-paper bin. 'Except that England is *not* a good idea with every copper in the land after my blood. And that this is as good a place as any from where to contact a few colleagues. Also, it's an easy drive from here to Switzerland, where I want to check out my account and make some fresh arrangements.'

She worked more solvent into a patch of beard.

'But I can hardly go to work here. I'm not set up for it. I could try, of course, but I'm sure to get nicked.'

He treated her tightly mini-skirted backside to a resounding slap. 'You, my darling, are going straight.'

She pouted. 'I shall get bored.'

'No you won't. For the moment you have Barcelona to explore. It's a wonderful city. Then, in a week or so perhaps, we might go down to the Costa del Sol, to Marbella. Soak up the sunshine. Meanwhile I shall be looking for an opening.'

She frowned at him. He was beginning to resemble some moth-eaten rat with his beard and moustache half off and the new growth beginning to appear. 'Opening?' she said. 'What do you mean, opening?'

'Funds are dwindling, Kirsty. All right, I have enough to keep us in luxury for two or three years . . .' – it was already understood, as much as if they had just got married, that they were going to stay together – 'but that does nothing but worry me. I would prefer to invest the funds in one big job to make enough to keep us for the rest of our lives. Settle down in the Caribbean somewhere, perhaps.'

She shook her head at him. 'No more terrorism, please?'

'Too dangerous. Terrorism is exactly the area they'll be looking for me. And there's sure to be some bastard ready to sell me out.' He smiled flatly at her. 'I was thinking about crime, *mi amor*. Good old-fashioned crime. A bank robbery perhaps. A bullion truck. The crown jewels. Who knows? Anything with a massive pay-off. I'm more prepared to pull something like that off than most of your common criminals – and I have some very experienced friends who I'm sure will be delighted to join me if I can come up with the right deal.' He grunted with pain once more as false whiskers came away, almost uprooting some fresh beard as they did. 'From now on I'm fishing, Kirsty – and you can fish with me.'

El Asesino would have been astounded to know that, within the short space of two hours, he was to stumble across the very idea that, successfully pulled off, stood to make him the fortune he was looking for. Or, rather, Kirsty was to unwittingly suggest it.

After lunch they took a table in the shade very close to the flat, where they ordered coffee and anis and settled down to watch the world go by. After a while, Arsenio left Kirsty to buy a newspaper. He bought a couple of magazines for her, one of them the sensational rag *Interviú*, noting as he did so that hard-core pornographic magazines – legal in Spain since shortly after the death of General Franco – such as the Swedish-owned *Private*, were not simply on sale, but were offered in great piles, albeit each little feast of porn was modestly shrink-wrapped. He was tempted to purchase one, then changed his mind; sex with Kirsty was dynamite, and some tawdry magazine or other was hardly going to improve it.

Settling down again with the newspaper *El País*, Arsenio felt relaxed and positively at home; sleazy the area might have been, but then he enjoyed that sort of ambience. The sun was bright and just short of hot, the shadow of the sunshade over their table made the temperature just perfect, and the sweet smell of orange blossom pervaded the air. With his false beard removed, he felt like a new man in his heavy black stubble. He had practically no fear of being recognized, having changed the colour of his eyes from luminous blue to pale brown with contact lenses, and slightly fattened his cheeks with wads of cotton wool – and even if some bright policeman did think he bore a passing resemblance to El Asesino, he was carrying his false Spanish national identity card complete with photograph and all the papers to back it up. Arsenio had merged perfectly into the seething bustle of Barcelona.

Lighting a Camel, he took two puffs at it, then, disgusted with himself and his lack of will-power where the deadly weed was concerned, he slung it to the pavement and ground it out with the sole of his shoe, angry with its hold over him.

An activity with which Arsenio was familiar, and which he always found entertaining, got under way

almost directly in front of them. He watched with
interest as a small, well-worn trestle-table was set
up on the flagstones. It was, of course, going to
be one of those floating – and illegal – gambling
games. A man in his thirties, a funny-looking
fellow with long, pointed sideboards and patchy
hair which looked as if it had been dyed black,
produced three halves of walnut shells and a
dried pea. He then proceeded to shift the inverted
nutshells and the pea around, covering the pea,
uncovering it, moving fast as a gypsyish-looking
woman clutching a fistful of paper money watched
him. For a while, neither of the two said a word;
nevertheless a few people gathered around, quietly
watching.

Arsenio left the table to get a closer look. He was
familiar with this scam, as he was with most – he
could even perform it – and he loved to watch it in
action. The woman, waving her bundle of money
around, began to encourage people to make bets
on which shell the little pea was under. Nobody
moved. Arsenio, vastly amused, waited for what
he knew was going to happen. And there she
was, he was sure of it – the third conspirator.
A typical overweight housewife or charlady in a
greasy apron. She produced a thousand pesetas
– and won her bet, doubling her money. She
bet the two thousand, won again, then she bet
the four, and won yet again. The small crowd
was growing, and the punter was communicating

her excitement. 'Come on, it's a doddle,' she was saying in Spanish. 'Anyone can beat this clown.' She added two thousand to the eight in her hand and then guessed the location of the pea correctly again, doubling the ten to twenty. When she wanted to bet the twenty it was refused and she went away, grumbling loudly about the unfairness of life.

Now that the shill – for shill she surely was – had departed, two men wanted to bet. The pea man let them both win a couple of times, then encouraged them to wager heavily – whereupon they lost. And that was the end of that pitch. A policeman was approaching, the table was folded up in a flash, and the team were on their way, some twenty-four thousand pesetas – £120 – richer, and all earned in ten minutes.

As Arsenio went back to the table and sat down, he was chuckling. 'God,' he said, 'people are such fools. The oldest scam in the world and they're falling for it all day, every day, all over the world.'

Kirsty grinned at him, flashing her perfect teeth. 'Sort of why I gave up making an honest living, darling,' she said. She had *Interviú* open at its centre pages. Passing it to him, she said, 'Will you look at this. Diana must be simply furious.'

He studied the photos. Diana on skis. Diana almost submerged. Carolyn Parker-Reed handing Diana her bikini top from the boat. Diana struggling aboard, sexy close-up of her bikinied bottom.

Her top coming loose. Close-up of the royal breasts. Arsenio smiled.

'Where were they taken?' asked Kirsty. 'What does it say?'

He told her, then he said, 'Just two days ago. They really rushed it in. Must have paid a fortune, She's a guest aboard a private cruise ship called the *Mirabelle*. The boat took off in a big hurry. Nobody knows where to.' He handed her back the magazine.

'They really hound the poor cow, don't they, those sons of bitches?' she observed, studying the pictures again.

'Good luck to them.'

'I don't see what's so sensational about a pair of tits. Even hers. Well, as long as they only take photographs I suppose it doesn't do her any real harm. They're not out to kidnap her or something.'

Arsenio grunted. He had been only half listening, his eyes on a busty, sexy, heavily painted young woman who was teetering by on six-inch stiletto heels in a tight little mini-skirt, and whom he was certain, judging by the size of her hands and feet, was a transvestite. He switched his attention back to Kirsty. 'Did you say something about kidnapping?'

'I said, at least no one's trying to kidnap Diana.'

'No.' An amused, thoughtful expression shadowed his face. 'Show me that again,' he asked, taking the magazine from her. He skipped through the prose. 'Heading north-west,' he muttered. 'Destination unknown.' He looked up at Kirsty. 'Which would mean, as a consequence of having been hounded by the rat-packs, that the *Mirabelle* is probably right now in very isolated waters.'

'Yes?'

'She sneaked out of England, it says. She was spotted at Stansted with just the kids and a friend, it says. That would mean she has no security men with her.'

'Yes?'

'She's somewhere, unprotected, on a luxury cruiser, off the coast of Spain, or maybe Portugal, or even France.'

'*Yes?*'

He glanced up at her from the magazine, his eyes deeply thoughtful. He fished in his pocket for some small change to settle the bill.

'Let's go upstairs and take a close look at my maps, shall we?' he said.

6

Joseph Hantash flew in from London that very evening, following a brief afternoon telephone conversation with Arsenio. He stayed the night in the Las Ramblas flat and by nine o'clock the next morning he and Arsenio were boarding a flight to Santander, a busy port in a heavily industrialized area, four hundred kilometres across the north of Spain from Barcelona. By ten-fifteen they were picking up the private helicopter which Arsenio had booked the previous afternoon by telephone, and by ten-forty they were airborne, just the two of them, Hantash at the controls.

Arsenio had decided it was unlikely that the *Mirabelle*, having, according to the *Interviú* report, made off in a north-westerly direction, had then turned around and headed north-east towards the coast of France. He told Hantash to fly west, following the spectacularly beautiful, rugged coastline of Asturias. Twenty minutes after take-off, when they reached Gijón and, just past it, Salinas – where the American tycoon's yacht had last been at anchor – the Palestinian headed north until they were some twelve kilometres into the Bay of Biscay. From there they followed the coastline more or less due west, at around 460 metres, their view encompassing all the shipping below them within a binocular range of more than seventy square kilometres.

They did not converse very much, these two highly trained terrorists bent on their first-ever wholly criminal enterprise. Hantash, who had unshakeable faith in Cruz Conde, and would join him at the crook of the Venezuelan's finger on any mission, nevertheless was harbouring the opinion that this latest idea was madcap from many angles. In the first instance, he doubted whether they would even discover the *Mirabelle*, never mind succeed in the wildly ambitious stunt of kidnapping no less a personage than the Princess of Wales. And yet since Arsenio was putting up all his expenses, Hantash was happy to go along with him, and was not about to express such misgivings.

Within an hour they had travelled two hundred kilometres and were passing Punta Candelaria on the coast, beginning to round the north-western tip of Spain, travelling south-south-west. They had seen only three large yachts, which might have been private cruise ships; one had turned out to be a ferry boat, the other two passenger-carrying pleasure cruisers. They had used up just over half a tank of fuel. Sixty kilometres further in, Arsenio told Hantash to turn inland to refuel at La Coruña airport. They were in a gloomy, polluted industrial area from where once, in 1588, the Spanish Armada had set sail for Britain and a routing by the British fleet commanded by Sir Francis Drake, and where now the sunshine filtered through a thin pall of smoke.

As the chopper's fuel tanks were being topped up, Hantash remarked, 'I don't like to say this, but it looks as if we are on a bit of a wild-goose chase. That ship could be anywhere, even headed for America. She might be way out in the Atlantic by now.'

'I doubt that,' said Arsenio. 'It's a family holiday. A rest. If Diana wanted to go to America she'd fly, my friend. But I figure that she'd want to move quite some way from where they were spotted.' He opened the map of the Iberian peninsula and its coastal waters. 'Look. What is it now – almost three days? The furthest they're likely to get at a comfortable cruising speed is . . .' – he traced his finger around the map – 'Lisbon. And I'm betting they haven't gone that far. I'm certainly not giving up until *we* have – maybe not even then.'

'Don't let it turn into an obsession, Arsenio.'

Arsenio considered that remark as Hantash restarted the rotor. The Palestinian was right, of course. As soon as the wild idea of kidnapping Lady Di had entered his head, it had lodged there, filling his mind; he had even dreamed about it last night. What fired him was more than the potentially massive financial reward of such an enterprise successfully carried out – it was the sheer enormous challenge of it, the excitement which made him feel he was living his corrupt lifestyle to the hilt. Almost two years without a woman had been easy to make up for. Two years without the rush of adrenalin which, curiously, lay beneath his outward icy calm when involved in something like the attack on the House of Lords, was more difficult to catch up on. Never mind the ransom money – he needed to tackle the huge problem of finding then kidnapping the Princess of Wales unharmed.

At that moment, the *Mirabelle* was far closer than Hantash – who actually did not believe they were going to find her – could possibly have imagined.

The yacht was in unusually calm Atlantic waters, at anchor just twelve nautical miles north-north-west of La Coruña, on the edge of busy fishing grounds. The boys were in the small pool on the main deck, and Diana was playing backgammon with Travers Bonnington, whose wife was sunbathing and chatting with Carolyn. Two stewards were beginning to lay a table for lunch, beneath colourful sunshades by the pool. It was a scene of super-rich, pampered tranquillity. At La Coruña airport, the man who was planning to wreck that tranquillity if he possibly could, was being airlifted once more by his hardened terrorist sidekick.

Fifteen minutes later, Diana, having just rolled the only combination of dice to beat her expert opponent in a game – a double six, thus eliciting a snort of disgust from her host and a giggle from her – looked up and towards the east, where the coastline of the province of Coruña was a thin, almost invisible smudge. There was the drone of an engine coming from that direction, getting louder, quite different from the chug of the distant fishing boats which were their only neighbours. She saw, high in the sky, a black dot getting larger by the second. As it became clear what that dot was, it was also apparent that it was descending.

'Shit, look at that,' said Diana.

'Helicopter. So what?' Bonnington, still miffed by that double six – though he knew he should not be, such were the sudden reversals of backgammon – did not look up from resetting his pieces for the next game.

'It's closing in on us,' Diana groaned, half a minute later. 'If it's *them* again, I'll damn well . . .' She failed to finish the sentence, but her host knew only too well who she meant, and sighed.

'Jackpot,' breathed Arsenio, eyes glued to his high-powered binoculars. 'We've hit the fucking jackpot. That, my friend, is the *Mirabelle*, and Diana's right there on deck, near the pool.' Lowering the binoculars, he made a note of the cruiser's

73

position. Then he said, 'Sheer off. Take a look at those fishing boats.'

'OK.' Hantash knew not to question the reason for that command.

Bonnington looked up from the board for the first time. 'They're turning away, Diana,' he remarked. 'There was no need to get your knickers in a twist, honey.'

The chopper had descended to less than two hundred metres. It was beginning to circle the fishing boats, some two kilometres distant.

'It's probably from the Ministry of Fisheries,' Bonnington offered. He rolled his dice and they bounced across the beautifully tooled leather surface of the Asprey's board. 'There's not exactly a war going on over there, but there's serious aggravation between the Brits, the French and the Spanish boats. Overfishing claims, illegal nets — that sort of stuff.'

Diana smiled. Her relief was obvious. 'Not to mention the Irish,' she said, well versed in the current situation.

'Why not? I'm half Irish myself. Your roll, I believe.'

One boat was heading away from the pack, low in the water with its heavy catch. Arsenio told Hantash to move the helicopter in close to her. She was Spanish, he saw, *La Señorita Juanita*, a ponderous drifter, some twenty metres long and broad of beam. There were six, sun-blackened men busy on her deck and all of them were staring at the chopper with hostile eyes – for there was indeed almost a fishing war going on out there and an intruder like the helicopter was regarded with the greatest of suspicion.

La Señorita Juanita, Arsenio saw, as his agile brain already began to form a plan, was from a place called Malpica – it was written on her weather-worn side in fading red letters, as was the name of its owners, 'Hmnos. Pomares', the Pomares brothers, and its registration number. He studied his map. Malpica was some eighteen sea miles to the west of La Coruña; it was a small town tucked in just before the point where the coastline went around a bend and dropped south towards Portugal. Satisfied, he told Hantash to climb to some 460 metres, then when, having circled for fifteen minutes with his eye on the now tiny trawler way below, he was satisfied that it was indeed heading for Malpica, he asked Hantash to turn inland for the town and look for some lonely spot as close as possible to it to put him down.

Arsenio's ingenious, reckless scheme was already almost fully mapped out in his head. It called for fast action, for he had no idea when the *Mirabelle* might head off, or when Diana would depart in its Dragonfly. Whatever happened, he figured, it would need tonight, all day tomorrow and tomorrow night to prepare for action on the following day. The risk that his bird would by then have flown was unavoidable. But at worst what he had in mind would cost him wages for Hantash, air fares and wages for two other key men, and the cost of the helicopter hire. At best it should net him in the region of ten million pounds.

Even as Hantash was setting him down on a bleak cliff top some three kilometres from Malpica, Arsenio was finishing outlining his plan to him and issuing his instructions.

As the helicopter took off again and headed back towards Santander, El Asesino, dressed only in a dark-blue T-shirt, jeans and white Reebok trainers, but carrying – as he always did – a great deal of cash, set off to walk along the cliff tops to Malpica, his brain racing.

7

Arsenio reached Malpica soon after two and,
sticking close to the beach, kept on walking along
the promenade of the rather sleepy, unimpressive
little fishing town until he came to the harbour. He
was hungry, and as yet the approaching dot at sea
which he assumed to be *La Señorita Juanita* was
distant enough for him to have time for a bite to
eat. Behind the harbour there was a café with an
assortment of *tapas* – tiny plates of fish, or meat,
or salad, meant to be washed down with a glass
of wine each. He was easy on the wine; he needed
to be as alert and quick-thinking as possible.

El Asesino's presence had excited little interest,
for Malpica also catered for a certain amount
of tourism – almost exclusively Spanish – and
strangers were commonplace. By the time he had
filled himself, *La Señorita Juanita* was nosing into
the harbour.

Pepe Pomares spared only a glance for Arsenio,
who was leaning against the sea wall of the
harbour, watching as two of his crew made his

drifter fast sideways against the ancient, worn and cracked harbour wall. Had Pomares been aware that this was the same man who had been in the helicopter which had been hovering over him almost two hours earlier he would have been convinced that Arsenio was an inspector from the Ministry of Fisheries. And he would have been rightly extremely concerned, for Pepe, the only survivor of the three Pomares brothers – one had drowned in a storm, the other had died of cancer – had been fishing with illegally large nets, ensuring a speedy and magnificent catch.

Arsenio studied the boat with covert interest. She was, as he had seen from the air, ideal for his purpose, just the right size and, most important of all, she was the genuine article. For the daring scheme which he had in mind, nothing but the real thing would do – a boat merely posing as a drifter would rapidly be singled out in the uproar unleashed by the kidnapping of the Princess of Wales.

Once *La Señorita Juanita* was made fast, the men got busy unloading their fish into trays of crushed ice which had been brought to the dockside in a battered old van. It was easy to see who the boss was, for the hefty Pepe Pomares was giving the orders. Once Arsenio had established who the skipper was, he drifted away, took a seat in the shade outside the café where he had had lunch – and waited.

An hour later, when Pomares left the harbour

on foot, Arsenio was following him at a discreet distance. He did not go far. Like most fishermen Pomares lived close to the harbour, in a tiny, end-of-terrace house no different from those of his crew. It was one street back from the promenade, with a small rose garden front and back, and on two floors. The front balcony boasted a large cage containing a cockatoo, and a smaller one with a pair of budgies.

'*Si?*' said Señora Pomares, an hour and a half later, a frown on her face as she opened her front door to a well-built stranger with a beard.

As there was no car-hire establishment in Malpica, Arsenio had taken a taxi to the larger inland town of Carbello, fifteen kilometres away, where he had rented a Seat Panda. Beforehand he had bought a slim briefcase, a clipboard, a pen and some sheets of white quarto paper, as well as a pair of blue cotton trousers, into which he had changed. He had covered a sheet of the paper with writing, and this, with blank ones beneath it, was attached to his clipboard, and the Panda was parked outside the door, when Señora Pomares stuck her nose out.

'Mrs Pomares?' asked Arsenio, studying his board.

'Yes,' she told him, suspiciously. She was a woman of about sixty with a grey, thin, worry-creased face, grey, piled hair to match, and she was wearing a dowdy, flower-print dress.

Arsenio flashed a confidence-winning smile. 'Congratulations,' he said. 'You have won a prize.'

'Prize?' she gaped at him. 'But I haven't entered any . . .'

Meanwhile he had unzipped the briefcase, and now produced a colourfully jacketed book on the art of cultivating roses. 'No,' he interrupted her, 'you have not entered a competition, but my company have a lottery of all the names in each town in Spain and you have won it in Malpica. He handed her the book.

'Well,' she said, turning it over in her gnarled hands – hands which might have belonged to a woman fifteen years her senior. 'That's very nice. But what company is it?'

'Encyclopaedia Britannica,' he said.

'Ah.' She studied him. 'You want to sell me some books, is that it? Well, thank you, no.' She tried to give him the book back, but he refused to take it.

'You keep that, whatever happens,' he told her. 'You don't have to buy anything. In fact, I want to give you, absolutely free, a brand-new video recorder.'

'What's that for, then?'

'You have children, Mrs Pomares?'

'Long since grown up and left, with children of their own.'

'You live alone, with your husband, then?'

Arsenio was oozing charm – had he wanted to lead a less dishonest life, he would surely have made a first-class salesman.

'I do – but I don't see what business that is of yours, I . . .'

'The children's encyclopaedia wouldn't interest you, then. But the adult one surely would. It comes in sixty-four wonderful, full-colour video tapes. Which is why we give you a video absolutely for nothing – so that you can enjoy them,'

'But, I'm sorry, I'm not interested in any encyclopaedia. Here, please take your book back.'

He ignored her offer. 'How can you know that my fine collection is not something that you would be proud to have in your house, and be fascinated by as you view it, until you've looked at a tape? Do you *have* a video machine, Mrs Pomares?'

'No.' She was beginning to turn stony.

'But you have a telly, right?'

'Yes, but . . .'

'I'll tell you what I'm going to do for you. Tomorrow evening – it can't be today, because I'm waiting for fresh supplies – tomorrow evening I'm going to bring you a video machine and one of the tapes. My technician will set it up for you. You and your husband watch the tape together. If you like what you see, I'll draw up a contract for the rest. It will cost you less than five thousand pesetas a month.' He produced a broad, friendly, honest smile. 'If you don't want the tapes, you just keep the video recorder. How does that sound?'

'What, *free*, a *video* recorder?'

'You heard correctly, Mrs Pomares.' He zipped up his briefcase, and began to turn away. 'Your husband will be here tomorrow evening, I take it?'

'He's just come back from a fishing trip. He doesn't go away again for a few days.'

'Good. Then you two decide, tomorrow evening, OK? No obligation whatsoever and, like I said, you keep the machine if you don't sign. OK? Do we have a deal, Mrs Pomares? Of course we do.'

Seconds later he was getting into his Panda with a friendly wave, leaving the woman staring after him with a surprised and puzzled expression on her face.

As he drove away, El Asesino glanced at his watch; there was still plenty of time to carry out stage two of the operation. He was well pleased with stage one. The Pomares woman would most certainly let him into her home the following evening. Now to get hold of an estate agent and find an isolated house to rent. Anywhere would do, so long as it was away from prying eyes.

A headquarters from which to run Operation Diana.

8

Hantash had been supplied by Arsenio with a list of ten men to begin trying to contact that afternoon as soon as he arrived back in Barcelona. Arsenio did not need ten men for the operation – he wanted five, including Hantash – but given the nature of these people, their various nationalities and the fact that most of them lived under false names, they were not going to be that easy to contact.

As it was, Hantash managed to reach only three. The first of these had not been far away. He was in Madrid and he hopped on a plane to Barcelona right away to arrive in the Las Ramblas flat by ten-thirty that night. He was a big, tough German called Felix Springer. No relation of the newspaper and magazine magnate Axel Springer, he was around forty. When in his early twenties, he had been one of the Baader–Meinhof terrorist group at the time of the infamous Schleyer kidnap and murder. When the German group disbanded, Springer began to operate as a freelance, as Arsenio had done for many years, and the two had met when working together for the Popular Front for the Liberation of Palestine. Like the other two men, who would not arrive until the following day, the German had not been told what the mission was to be; the fact that he had been asked to come to Barcelona to join El Asesino for what had been described to him over the telephone by Hantash as 'an interesting little enterprise' was quite enough for him.

Kirsty, relishing this entirely unexpected and welcome change in her life – for she needed excitement every bit as much as her lover – was in buoyant mood as she rustled up a steak for the hungry German. She rather liked his rugged looks, and she was bubbly towards him, smiling a lot, joking. She meant nothing by this beyond a welcoming friendliness, but she had failed to consider – and she was wearing a revealing blouse and mini-skirt – what sort of effect her amiable attitude might have on the man. Had either she or Hantash told Springer what her relationship was with Arsenio, then he would certainly have made no move in her direction. But neither of them thought to, and she was merely introduced as Kirsty. So when she went off to bed alone, having treated Springer to the sweetest of smiles – and then Hantash showed him where he was to sleep, in a single bed in a small room with him – the German entirely misinterpreted Kirsty's friendliness. He was sure she had been showing out to him – and that was entirely, albeit unwittingly, her fault.

It was a very warm night. Kirsty had drunk three vodka tonics, plus some wine with her meal and when, after midnight, she went to bed, she was very tired. She stripped back the sheet – there was no need for one in Barcelona at that time of year – took all of her clothes off, flopped gratefully on to the bed and immediately fell asleep.

The first she knew of the fact that there was someone else in her room was when Springer's big hand closed over her breast. He was also naked. Her bare body, vaguely visible in the light from a street lamp creeping through a crack in the curtains, he took as confirmation that he was making no mistake in this intrusion. Hantash had gone down for a drink in the still busy Las Ramblas and the German had seized the opportunity immediately, only five minutes after Kirsty had retired. He assumed that Kirsty was awake and eagerly awaiting him.

Heavy with sleep, she half awoke to find Springer's big erection digging into the top of the side of her thigh and his other hand slipping flatly over her stomach, its fingers sliding into her pubic bush. Thinking he was Arsenio, she reached for his hard-on and fisted it. It was only when she completely woke up and he grunted something guttural in German that she realized the appendage did not belong to her lover – it was too thick – and that in any case Arsenio was not in the house.

She screamed. Shocked, Springer clamped a hand over her mouth. 'What is the matter?' he asked, without slackening his hand.

Releasing his penis, she thumped him solidly in the testicles with the side of her closed fist. Letting go of her mouth, he groaned, rolled away from her and doubled up.

'What the hell do you think you're doing?' she yelled at him as she dragged the sheet over herself.

'But I thought you, I thought you . . .' he gasped, clutching his testicles in both hands.

'You must be crazy, Felix. Don't you know I'm Arsenio's woman?'

'Arsenio's?' He turned his head to her. 'Ah, shit. Shit. I am sorry. I was thinking that you was, you was hot for – what is it – a poking, you know?'

Now that she realized the man was not trying to rape her, she saw the funny side. The way he had expressed himself made her want to giggle – an impulse she stifled. 'You'd better get out of here,' she told him.

Still holding himself, he sat up and swung his legs off the bed. 'You will not tell him?' he asked her. 'It was really some big mistake. I do not mess with my friends, their womens, you know?'

'I'll only tell him if I want you dead,' she said, only her head and the tips of her fingers visible over the sheet.

'But you do not want this thing?'

'I won't tell him, clown. Now get your arse out of here and let me sleep.'

She even watched that faintly illuminated, heavily muscled bare backside with a certain amount of prurient interest as the German hurried from her bedroom. Then, a smile on her face, she slipped the sheet off, turned on her side and went straight back to sleep. She had been lucky that she was Arsenio's girlfriend – for Felix Springer had a history of rape and, excited as he had been, would almost certainly have raped her had she not been.

Kirsty made certain the following day, as each of the other two of Arsenio's little gang showed up, to tell them that she was the boss's girl and so it was strictly hands off. The first to arrive was the Irishman Tim Shannon, who had left a contact number in Dublin after parting with Arsenio in London only a few days ago after the escape. The second, who turned up at lunch-time, was an extremely useful Syrian gentleman whose name was Salim Kasar. Forty-two years old – Arsenio wanted experienced men with him, not young hotheads – Kasar at the age of twenty had been a trainer of terrorist methods in Libya when such different factions as the Red Army, the PLO, even the IRA, had been training together. He did regular heavy exercise and was as fit as any man half his age. He was also, as were all four of Arsenio's recruits – even the Irishman, whose remarks often failed to bear this out – highly intelligent.

By teatime the four of them – a disappointed Kirsty was left behind because there was no way Arsenio was going to have a woman on this deal despite her having begged him before he left, and then again, that very afternoon on the telephone – were boarding a plane in Barcelona. At six-fifteen, Arsenio picked them up at La Coruña.

It was fortunate that they carried little luggage besides jeans and T-shirts and a few special items which Hantash had picked up from a sports shop and from an underground contact of El Asesino in Barcelona, for four big, heavy men fit into a Panda as tightly as playing cards in their box.

By seven they were in an isolated holiday cottage on the banks of the wide River Allones, some seventeen kilometres from Malpica.

It was light in that part of the world in mid-July until almost nine-thirty, and encyclopaedia salesman Arsenio Cruz Conde was not planning on taking his technician to install a video machine in the Pomares' little house near the harbour until night descended.

9

'Oh. So it's *you* again.' Señora Pomares had opened her door just enough to see out. In the pool of light which emerged from her living-room stood Arsenio. Just behind him, a large cardboard box in his arms, was Shannon.

'Naturally it is me, madam. I never miss an appointment,' said Arsenio. 'I've brought you your video and not one, but two tapes. And as I told you, you are under no obligation to enter into a contract. My man will install the video and – as I promised you – it is yours whether you decide to enter into a contract with us or not.'

'There has to be a catch somewhere. It's too good to be true,' came a gruff voice from within, louder than that from the television, which was showing a word game called *Lingo*.

The fisherman's wife opened the door wider, as at the same time she flung over her shoulder, 'But where can there be a catch, Pepe? This man, he is going to plug the machine in and leave it with us. He can't force us to sign a cheque, now can he?'

Arsenio put a foot in the door. 'May we come in then, please, Mrs Pomares?' he said, most pleasantly. 'This won't take more than ten minutes.'

'Can they come in, Pepe?' she asked.

'But I am not turning the telly off. You know this is my favourite programme.'

'We won't need to turn it off, sir,' Arsenio called out.

'All right, come in.'

It was a typical working-class living-room, chintzy, with flowered wallpaper and a huge, walnut-coloured, glass-fronted cabinet – too big by far for the room – filled with bric-à-brac and a heavy-patterned dinner service with enough plates to feed an army. Three brightly coloured china ducks were flying across one wall, at odds with the paper, and a big, gilt-framed painting of the haloed Virgin Mary adorned another.

As Señora Pomares closed the door, Shannon was putting the cardboard box down on the lace-edged runner of the dining-room table. Opening one end, he slid his hand in. When he removed it he was holding a Smith & Wesson 459 handgun fitted with a silencer. He had passed this to Arsenio and taken another out for himself before either of the Pomares realized what was happening. The woman was the first to notice. As she screamed, Arsenio turned up the volume of the television.

The expression on the fisherman's crumpled, weather-beaten face hardly changed. 'We have nothing of any value,' he said firmly. 'Why are you doing such a thing in the home of a God-fearing man?'

'But indeed you have something of value to us,' Arsenio told him. '*La Señorita Juanita*.'

'My boat? Why would you take my old boat? To you she is worthless, for I can see you are no fisherman. And where would you sell her? To me, she is my livelihood. Why do you want to take away from me my bread and my wine?'

The woman had sunk down into the chair and was quietly sobbing. She seemed to have shrunk in size, and looked even older.

'I am not going to take your boat from you,' said Arsenio. There was no menace in his voice; the guns provided all the intimidation necessary. 'I am going to borrow it for a while. Providing you cooperate with me in every way I demand, you will come to no harm. Neither will your wife – or the boat.'

Arsenio approached Señora Pomares to lay a hand, from which she flinched away, on her shoulder. 'We are not going to hurt you,' he told her. 'But I'm afraid we are going to have to take you away for a short while.'

She wailed. 'Away?' said the fisherman. 'What do you mean by that?'

'We need some insurance, Pepe. I have to be certain that you will not double-cross us.' He waved the pistol under the man's nose. 'Please get up. Take

91

me into your kitchen.' On the television, Ramoncín, the bright young host of *Lingo*, had just persuaded a pair of middle-aged contestants to go for doubling the prize of over a million pesetas they had just won. They lost the lot, and Ramoncín was being his charmingly sympathetic self while no doubt pleased to have saved the company more than two million '*pelas*', as he called them.

The advertising break came up, the volume even louder. The Irishman turned it down now that Señora Pomares was merely quietly blubbering.

In the kitchen, Arsenio, not relishing the necessary role of scaring a couple who were almost at retirement age, said to the man, 'Your wife does not have to be told the danger she will be in. She is going to be moved to a place where no one would think of looking for her. She is going to be well looked after, she will not be hurt in any way – that is, so long as you cooperate with us.' He stared hard at the man, putting on his fiercest expression. 'However, should you give us the slightest problem, she *will* be hurt. Do you follow me?' The man nodded stonily. 'And if you give us a major problem,' Arsenio added, 'we may be obliged to cripple her.' He helped himself to a glass of water.

'I shall give you no shit problem,' said Pomares. 'Just tell me why it is you want the use of my good boat?'

'One moment. Come with me.'

Taking the man back into his living-room, he

said to his wife, 'When you leave here, old one, you will be making no fuss. You will go perfectly quietly. You will not be ill-treated in any way.' He rammed the silencer under her husband's chin. 'Should you make an attempt to run, or to call for help, I shall . . .' – he pointed the Smith & Wesson at Pomares' legs – 'first cripple him in the knee. If your resistance continues I shall . . . I shall perhaps be obliged to kill him – and you. You do understand?'

The woman's blubbering grew louder again. Her frail shoulders were shaking as she sat hunched into a protective ball on her chair. Arsenio had it within him to feel sorry for her, but he made no room for such a sentiment.

'Impress on her that she has to pull herself together,' he said to the fisherman. 'That she is to leave this house for a while – and perfectly quietly – come what may. That if you behave correctly then neither of you will be any the worse once this is over. I may even decide to compensate you for your inconvenience.'

'Like the free video?' said the ageing seafarer wryly.

'We shall see.' Arsenio's hand went back to the woman's shoulder, gently. 'Tell her in your own way,' he said to the man. 'We don't have all night.'

It took almost half an hour before Señora Pomares was sufficiently resigned to the fact that

93

she was to be forcibly taken off somewhere to accept it calmly. Outwardly composed, but terrified within, she walked erectly with Shannon down her little path and ducked quietly into the passenger seat of the Panda. Shannon took a mobile telephone from the glove compartment and showed it to her. Arsenio had already displayed the telephone that had been in the cardboard box with the guns and told her that the Irishman would call if she started to make trouble – and that her husband's kneecap would be shattered with a bullet.

She sat in the Panda, utterly silent and shrivelled, a petrified mouse, as Shannon drove them through Malpica and off on a country road towards the Río Allones. In the little house, El Asesino opened a bottle of the fisherman's table wine and, sharing it with him, settled down to watch – for the third time in his life – one of his favourite films, which Tele 5 happened to be showing that evening. It was *The Good, the Bad and the Ugly*, with Clint Eastwood.

They showed up in that tiny rented car, the three big men, at two-thirty in the morning. The broad-shouldered Joseph Hantash, Felix Springer and Salim Kasar, together with Arsenio Cruz Conde, and the fisherman himself, seemed to almost fill the small living-room. They were dressed in faded T-shirts, scruffy jeans and rubber boots. Springer, being the only one of the three with a pale complexion, had turned his face dark with instant suntan oil. They had brought jeans, a faded denim shirt and rubber boots for Arsenio to change into, a large, heavy duffle bag, and a flight bag full of provisions.

A short while later, when Arsenio was ready, they left the house. Hantash locked the Panda and they all trooped quietly down, with Pepe Pomares, through dark and silent streets to the harbour.

It was a warm, still night. The scent of night-flowering jasmine lay sweetly heavy in the air. Somewhere a pair of cats were fighting; apart from that, the only sound was the rushing noise of long, flat waves as they swept majestically over the beach. Overhead, a sliver of moon, smudged with barely moving wisps of cloud, hung in a brilliant bed of stars.

La Señorita Juanita, as the five men approached her, appeared as a black shadow in smooth, dark waters that reflected the stars. Nothing stirred in the harbour apart from the phoney fishermen and their genuine, if coerced, captain as they boarded the drifter. They were all being as quiet as possible as Pomares issued instructions on how to cast off the boat, and Arsenio translated them. Within fifteen minutes, the hijacked boat, its navigation lights twinkling, engines chugging, was slipping out of the waters of Malpica harbour towards the distant fishing grounds, near which, Arsenio fervently hoped, the *Mirabelle*, with her ten-million-pound prize, was lying at anchor.

Aboard that luxury cruiser, in bed in her private suite, the boys sleeping in an adjoining cabin, the Princess of Wales was peacefully dreaming.

10

By first light, *La Señorita Juanita* was surrounded by – though the intervening distances were considerable – a host of other fishing boats. They were Spanish, they were French, they were British and they were Irish – all here to fish these rich waters. It was essential that El Asesino and company appeared to be as busy and as genuine as everybody else, and to that effect they went through the arduous business of putting out the drift-nets. When that was done, Arsenio settled down within the squarish, high-built iron bridge of the boat with his binoculars trained on the *Mirabelle*, where breakfast was just being served.

'I think I should like to go home soon, Mother,' said Prince William, just turned thirteen, through a mouthful of bacon and egg.

Ten-year-old Harry gravely agreed with him; a yacht, however luxurious and well supplied with games and videos and other things to do, was too confining for growing boys. They were getting bored, missing their friends.

Diana had been expecting this to happen sooner or later. She and her hosts, it seemed, were the only ones who were not getting bored, for Carolyn had been grumping to her the previous evening; but then the daughter of the Home Secretary was a highly sexed young lady who was craving the attentions of her latest boyfriend. Diana sniffed; all this swimming, sun and relaxation had brought on a cold. Personally she could have stayed out here away from the hustle and bustle of her life – and the pestilential paparazzi – for another month at least. But she had to consider her children. Carolyn, of course, was free to leave in order to slake her sexual appetite any time she wanted, but Diana did not want the boys to travel home without their mother.

'Well, all right,' she said grudgingly. 'Let's enjoy one more day's sunshine and then leave tomorrow.' She glanced at her host, who was swamping a thin slice of toast with lashings of thick marmalade. 'Is that OK with you, Travers?' she asked.

'My chopper's at your service any time you want, honey,' he drawled. 'But we'll be sorry to see you go. Kids seldom stay the course aboard, and I understand why.'

'Tomorrow, then. Super,' said Carolyn, blue eyes shining. 'I must call David after breakfast.'

Pomares' boat, with its long line of blue-painted cork floats stretching behind it as far as the' eye could see, had been slowly drifting with a not particularly strong current all morning as its nets began to fill with fish. By eleven o'clock it was further away from the *Mirabelle* than suited Arsenio's purpose and he told Pomares to start the engines and move back towards the yacht until they were just close enough to pick up any movement on her decks without binoculars.

Hantash was on watch when a small boat began to be winched down to the sea with people aboard. He picked up the binoculars and studied it until it was afloat and free.

'This is it,' he called out excitedly to Arsenio. 'She's going swimming with the boys.'

Arsenio smiled. 'Action stations,' he said. 'Let's do it.'

She liked to dive down deep, as deep as she could go, then let herself drift to the surface, holding her breath until she was almost there, enjoying the unreal sensation of being completely and utterly cut off from the entire world while she did this, then claw herself over the side of the speedboat to stand on its prow and dive cleanly in once again. She was happily topless, a golden brown all over, a skimpy white bikini bottom her only item of clothing.

As she knifed into the sun-drenched waters for the third time, sinking like a stone, she failed to realize she had company other than the fish until a big, strong hand grabbed hold of her upper arm. The shock was tremendous. She thought at first that she had been seized by a shark, or a killer whale, and that she was as good as dead. Then she saw, but vaguely for she was down deep enough for the sun to be only weakly penetrating the sea, that a man had taken hold of her. A man equipped with an aqualung and breathing mask. As she struggled, another scuba diver came up on her opposite side and her other wrist was taken in a savage grip, the arm was forced behind her back in a half nelson, and a breathing mask was slipped over her head. Terrified, helpless to put up more than a token resistance, she found herself being forced flat in the water. Now facing downwards, her arms in a full nelson, the hands bent painfully up into the back of her neck, she was sandwiched between the two divers.

The men had C212 Mercury scuba-jet motors strapped to their stomachs. Felix Springer, whose career to date had included a stint as a deep-sea diver in the North Sea, was carrying an extra oxygen cylinder on his back, and it was to this that the face mask which had been thrust over the woman's face was attached.

El Asesino, the other aggressor, had thought this operation out in most meticulous detail, down to the fact that there were large plastic bags attached to the outlets of the face masks so that there would be no tell-tale signs of bubbles streaming up to the surface.

It was the perfect snatch; perfect but for one fact,

which Arsenio realized at the moment he seized the woman's arm, a fact which filled him with fury and rage towards Hantash. Of course, he should never have let anyone else take over the surveillance. He should only, ever, trust himself in these matters. For the young woman they had captured was not Lady Diana Spencer, Princess of Wales – it was her companion, whose name at that moment escaped him, though he remembered having seen her picture in *Interviú*.

Well, he thought, a madness seething within him as the scuba jets towed the three of them swiftly back in the direction of *La Señorita Juanita*, he had blown it and it was his stupid fault for delegating a crucial part of the operation. As soon as he had realized he did not have Diana, he also understood that the mission would be aborted whether or not he let this female go. If he did release her, his bird would be warned and would fly out of there *prontissimo* in the Bonnington chopper; if he did not, the area would shortly be teeming with people searching for a body.

He would have to settle for the woman they were dragging through the sea between them. So, she was not Diana and he had lost the challenge to himself, the idea which had filled him with fire – but all the same she was surely excellent kidnap material.

Carolyn Parker-Reed, meanwhile, was fighting more than her terror. She had never got on with face masks and scuba diving, she'd been unable to master the special technique for breathing and, despite a plentiful supply of oxygen, she felt she was choking. Together that dreadful sensation and her fear caused her to pass out.

'She should have come up by *now*,' said Prince William as he and Prince Harry anxiously searched the water with their eyes. 'She never stays down this long.'

'Perhaps she swam under the yacht?' suggested Harry. 'Maybe she's on the other side of it?'

'That must be it, yes,' William agreed. The *Mirabelle* was looming above them. He called out three times for his mother before she appeared at the ship's rail.

'*What?*' exclaimed Diana at her eldest son's question. '*Christ!*' She sprinted around the yacht, hoping to God that she would find her friend swimming on the other side of it. When she did not, beginning to panic, she tore back until she was again above the boys. Still seeing no sign of Carolyn, she screamed, loudly enough for the entire boat to hear, '*Help!* Carolyn's *missing!*'

The Princess of Wales, wearing a halter top and shorts, kicked off her shoes and plunged into the sea.

'You ballsed up, Joe, you unbelievably stupid *bastard*,' snarled Arsenio as Hantash took hold of one of the unconscious Carolyn's forearms and

Salim Kasar the other and they hauled her up into the fishing boat.

'What?' retorted Hantash, not comprehending. Carolyn's chin was lolling into her chest, and her short hair, plastered to her head, was indistinguishable from that of Diana. Until she was on her back on the deck, and he removed her oxygen mask, Hantash failed to realize that she was not Lady Di. Then he said, 'Shit, man, you got the wrong woman,' which remark added fuel to Arsenio's anger as he dragged himself up over the side.

'You're supposed to be a crack operator. You *are* a crack operator. How can you make such a dumb mistake?'

Hantash shrugged. He was not used to being spoken to like this, and it was irritating him. 'They look alike, don't they? She was with the boys. How was I to know? Christ.'

Arsenio stalked up on to the bridge, grabbed the binoculars and brought them down. He scanned the area of the *Mirabelle*, picking up the speedboat. Diana had just come up alongside, her face filled with horror. There were now several men, including Travers Bonnington, in the sea, diving, searching. Arsenio thrust the binoculars into Hantash's hands. 'Look,' he snarled. 'Look well. There's no mistaking her, even at this distance. Arsehole.'

The Palestinian fought back his anger, turning it on himself. Arsenio was right: the women might be similar in appearance, but they were nevertheless distinctive. He had been sloppy, totally careless — an attitude which one day might cost him his life. Yet he did not excuse himself, but merely handed the binoculars back, glowering.

Carolyn's eyes flickered open. She thought for a moment she had been having a bad dream. Then she saw the men standing over her, two in rubber boots, two in scuba gear, one of them unstrapping a scuba jet from his waist — his gaze fixed pruriently on her bare breasts. She covered them with her hands, then tried to say something, but her lips were trembling so much she could produce only unintelligible sounds.

Arsenio meanwhile went back to the bridge and got hold of Kirsty in Barcelona on his mobile phone and asked her to check in *Interviú* who this young woman was. It took only moments. When he came back down on to the deck, Carolyn was sitting up, forearms folded over her breasts, head in hands. He picked up his denim shirt from where it lay nearby and draped it over her shoulders. He crouched beside her, his head close to hers.

'It was a mistake,' he told her. 'An error. We were after Diana, do you see? Because I have a fool working for me, we got you instead.'

'Lay off me, Arsenio,' growled Hantash.

'Yeah.'

Carolyn, tears mixed with the sea water on her

cheeks, turned her face to look at him. She managed to speak, falteringly.

'You, then . . . you will, you *will* let me go?' she mumbled.

'I'm afraid not, no. You see, I know who you are. You're Carolyn Parker-Reed. Your dad's Stephen Parker-Reed, the British Home Secretary. He's also a multimillionaire – and this is a kidnapping. You'll have to do in place of Diana, Carolyn.'

She wailed, then buried her head in her hands once again.

'I'm not going to hurt you. But you're going to have to be with us for some while. And you're going to be uncomfortable, but you'll have to put up with it.' He nodded at Springer. 'Get her below.'

Uncomfortable was an understatement. She was too distraught to notice that it was no accident that the big German groped both her breasts when, having pulled her to her feet, he took her by the armpits and lowered her through an open hatch of the hold. The hatch was closed on her and she was in darkness, the slowly rolling and creaking wooden hull slippery beneath her bare feet, the air filled with the stink of stale fish. Folding herself into a foetal ball, Carolyn began to sob.

'She's drowned,' Travers Bonnington pronounced as he pulled himself into the speedboat. 'We have to face it – the poor girl has drowned.'

Diana was utterly distraught. 'But how is that

possible?' she protested. 'She's an excellent swimmer. She couldn't just *drown*.'

Bonnington put an arm around her shoulders. 'She's gone, Di.'

'A shark. God, it must have been a *shark*.' Her face was ravaged, tears were streaming down it.

'There would be signs. Blood. No, something else must have happened. A heart attack.'

'Then why doesn't she, why doesn't she, she . . . *float*?'

'It must have been so severe the spasm knocked all the air out of her.' The American sighed heavily. 'I'd better get back aboard and call her father.'

11

Stephen Parker-Reed was in excellent spirits. He had just had a most rewarding private meeting with the Prime Minister, who had praised him highly for his recent handling of a most alarming threat by the Metropolitan Police to go on strike, and he was now making arrangements for his planned holiday in the Bahamas.

The Home Secretary, a man as lean as the hatstand which stood in the corner of his office, with a sunken, ascetic face and a bald head fringed with a slight smudge of thin grey hair, allowed himself a rare indulgence for a working day; he produced a bottle of Glenfiddich malt whisky, and a heavy, cut-lead-crystal tumbler from a drawer in his antique desk, poured himself a respectable measure, admired its colour for a moment, sniffed it, then took a generous sip. The malt slipped down his throat as smoothly as honey, to hit his stomach warmly in just the right spot. Leaning back in his leather-padded swivel chair, he peered through his first-floor sash window. Raindrops were trickling down it; it had been drizzly for days. Well, he would very shortly, like his daughter on Travers Bonnington's boat off the north of Spain, be soaking up the sunshine. How he was looking forward to a well-deserved rest.

It was curious that he should have been thinking of his daughter and their American friend at the very moment when his secretary put Bonnington through to him on the telephone. When the brief, awful conversation was over, Parker-Reed was a shattered man.

For long minutes, his grief was so overwhelming that he could do nothing but cry; he did not even touch his whisky. Then, making a massive effort to pull himself together, he drained the malt in one, splashed more into the glass, and told his secretary to put him through to a close friend of his, Royal Navy Admiral of the Fleet Sir Julian Oswald, GCB. His daughter's life having come to a most tragic finish, the least he could do was to ensure divers made a thorough search for her body so that she could be brought home for a decent Christian burial.

The Type-23 frigate *Argyll* was the closest vessel of HM Fleet to the coast of La Coruña at that particular time. She was on exercise off the southernmost Spanish province to the north of Portugal, Pontevedra. At full speed she would reach the *Mirabelle* in little over three hours.

*　　*　　*

Arsenio, having worked out one plan of action as far as a ransom demand for the Princess of Wales was concerned, was now obliged to adapt this for the daughter of the Home Secretary. But he was in no hurry to put it into operation. Certainly, he should let several hours go by before revealing that Carolyn was a kidnap victim and not drowned – enough time, that was, for the police to assume she had been taken a great distance from the site of the undersea abduction.

He had made the young woman as comfortable as possible by supplying her with a blanket to lie on and the jeans and thin sweater he had thought to bring along for his royal target. Nevertheless, the rolling of the drifter – they were in a swell which had been having almost no effect on the massive *Mirabelle* – combined with the sickly, suffocating stale-fish smell in the unventilated hold, was making her feel queazy. She had no watch; she guessed, after three hours, that she had been a prisoner in that stinking place – into which barely enough light filtered for her to see her hand in front of her face – for twice as long. The terror had left her. She had rationalized that this swarthy, bearded man, who was clearly the boss, was being as kind as he could to her, that he was only after money which her father would surely come up with, that there was nothing for it but to steel herself for a lengthy ordeal.

Carolyn was vomiting in a corner of the hold

when El Asesino spotted HMS *Argyll* closing in on the *Mirabelle*. The fishing boat had drifted to over three kilometres away from the yacht by then, but Arsenio's glasses were powerful enough, even at that distance, to make out that a Royal Navy frigate had appeared on the scene, and that frogmen were going over its side. He was impressed; if such was the power of the Home Secretary, then such would be his capacity to come up with the ransom money. Arsenio had decided that while the nice, round figure of £10,000,000 for a personage as important as HRH the Princess of Wales was about right, perhaps that sum was overambitious and would complicate the matter as far as her friend was concerned.

Even as he was watching the divers go about their abortive task, he decided on five million instead. He could, of course, have the divers called off by making one simple telephone call. But no, he told himself, it was too soon to play his hand and in any case it amused him that his action was causing so much activity. His anger had subsided, yet he remained intensely irritated that he had not pulled off the kidnap of the century.

Stephen Parker-Reed took a private jet at his disposal down to La Coruña, where he was picked up by Bonnington's helicopter and flown to the *Mirabelle*. He was on board by five in the afternoon, to be greeted by the depressing news that his daughter's body had not been found and that it was doubtful that it would be.

Arsenio observed the departure and return of the chopper with great interest. When he saw a single passenger emerge, he guessed correctly who that tall, thin and stooping figure had to be, finding it ironic that he should have kidnapped the daughter of the very man ultimately responsible for the maintenance of law and order in Great Britain. Arsenio's spirits were beginning to pick up; receiving £5,000,000 from such a personage was going to prove almost as satisfying as extracting £10,000,000 from the royal family itself.

Six hours had elapsed since the snatch. Time enough. He would put the Home Secretary out of his misery. Before even leaving Barcelona on his search for the *Mirabelle*, Arsenio had checked out the yacht's telephone number via the London shipping directories. He called Kirsty, at home in Las Ramblas awaiting her first instructions on her contribution to the cause.

When she completely understood the situation, and what she was to do, Kirsty hung up, left the flat and took a taxi to the telephone exchange. While it was impossible that this initial call could be traced, it was almost certain that future ones – whether to the *Mirabelle*, the Home Office or Parker-Reed's private house – would be. The man, Arsenio was sure, was not going to part with his money without a struggle, a certain amount of stalling was sure to be involved — it invariably was in kidnap cases — and traces would be put on all calls. Best for Kirsty to get into the habit right away of calling from public telephones.

The ship's captain took Kirsty's call. Excitedly, he passed it down from the bridge to the luxurious stateroom, where Parker-Reed, weighed down with his grief, was trying to drown it in Bonnington's best malt.

'We have Carolyn,' Kirsty told him. 'She's safe and she's well.'

The Home Secretary's face underwent a miraculous transformation. The years it seemed to have put on during the morning faded away. 'But, but . . . why? *How*?' he stuttered.

'Money, Mr Parker-Reed. She's been kidnapped and she won't be harmed in the slightest providing you cooperate.' Kirsty was rather enjoying her new role. She even sounded rather chirpy on the line.

'Let me talk to her.'

'She's not here. She's somewhere where she will never be found. Don't even try to look. Deliver the money when and how you are instructed and you'll get her back.' Through the glass window of her booth, Kirsty was watching a teenager having a row with his girlfriend in the bustling exchange. A fat woman was selling flowers from a stall in the corner. Kirsty felt unreal delivering these words while surrounded by normal, everyday life.

'How much do you want?' At the other end of

the line the Home Secretary did not feel particularly
real either. His drowned daughter suddenly wasn't,
his life was not, after all, destroyed – for Carolyn
was his life, as his wife had died the year before
and there were no other children. Money, at that
moment, was his last consideration. His question
was put to the faceless female voice as if he were
asking the price of a painting.

But when Kirsty told him £5,000,000, the sum
suddenly loomed vast before his eyes – great sacks
of money, a fortune.

'You can't be serious?'

'You want to see your daughter alive, don't you,
Mr Parker-Reed, now that you know what it was
like when you thought she was dead?' The script
had been written for Kirsty by Arsenio.

'That sort of money in cash is going to take some
while to get together.'

'Of course it is. We know that. We have plenty
of time. As long as it takes.'

Parker-Reed sighed heavily. 'Very well. How . . .?'

Kirsty interrupted him. 'That's all for now. Stay
on the boat. I'll be in touch in two hours' time. By
the way, just to impress on you that you're not
dealing with amateurs. Carolyn is in the hands of
Arsenio Cruz Conde, El Asesino. I'm sure you've
heard of him – he's the one who just sprung himself
from Parkhurst.' She hung up.

Kirsty seriously doubted the wisdom of making
that last statement, but Arsenio had insisted. He

had, he had told her over the phone when she had protested, nothing to lose. Anyway, the whole world was after him. Let them sit up and take notice. And the knowledge would certainly convince Stephen Parker-Reed to cough up in the shortest possible time.

Operation Diana may have been aborted, but Operation Carolyn was well underway.

12

'She's alive, Travers. She's alive.' Parker-Reed's greyish-blue eyes had tears in them.

'*What*? But . . . that, that's wonderful.' Bonnington frowned. It made no sense. Her death had turned his friend's head. 'So where the hell is she then?'

'I don't know. She's been kidnapped.'

'You're joking. How is that possible? She vanished from under the sea.'

The Home Secretary's face creased with worry again. 'I don't know. But she's in the hands of El Asesino. The terrorist.'

'Jesus. I've heard of him, of course.' Then it was true. Carolyn was alive. Stephen had not gone nuts. 'Didn't he just go on the run from one of your prisons?' he asked.

'Escape-proof Parkhurst, yes. And just a few days ago. How he set this up so quickly beats me.'

The American thought for a moment. 'He was after Diana, of course. But how in hell . . .?'

They told Diana the astonishingly good – yet

nevertheless frightening – news, then they called the boys to the stateroom and questioned them closely. Surely there must have been a boat nearby when Carolyn disappeared? No, not that they had seen, said the boys. Unless it was on the other side of the *Mirabelle*. Something under the sea, then? Did they notice a strange shape, perhaps? Nothing.

'Just a second,' said Parker-Reed when the boys had gone, 'how could Arsenio have known I was aboard – unless he had been watching?' He went to a window. The big fleet of fishing boats from several countries had drifted so far they were little more than dots on the horizon. The *Argyll*, already heading back south, was approaching them. 'Those fishing boats were much closer to us when I arrived.'

'They're drifters. They only use their engines when they're beginning to slip away from the fish. Are you suggesting that this Arsenio guy is aboard one of them?'

'Sounds pretty far-fetched, doesn't it? But he's somewhere – and he's got my daughter, damn him. I'd like to speak to the man who took the telephone call first from that woman.'

Captain Bland had a keen memory. 'Her first words were, "We have Carolyn Parker-Reed", sir,' he said. 'Naturally, I was overjoyed.' He hastily qualified that remark. 'That she was alive, sir.'

'And then?' The Home Secretary asked him.

'She said she wanted to get directly in touch

with yourself, sir. Could I get your number from the yacht's owner? Of course, I told her that you were aboard.'

Arsenio had worked this little possible give-away out for himself. He was having no further slip-ups.

'Ah. Well, thank you.'

When the captain had gone, Parker-Reed, back at a window and watching the distant boats – the *Argyll* was passing them to the south – said, 'Just the same, she could be out there somewhere. Do you mind if I use your phone?'

'You Brits are unbelievable. Of course you can use the goddam phone.'

He got through to Admiral Sir Julian Oswald and told him all that had happened, thanking him for sending the *Argyll* so promptly. He suggested it might be a good idea if the Royal Navy frigate nosed about a bit among the fishing boats.

It was several seconds before Sir Julian replied. 'Not on, I'm afraid, old boy. Tensions are pretty high among the fishermen at the moment. There's been a lot of funny business going on. Accusations of fishing within other people's territorial waters, illegally large nets – that sort of thing. Almost a repetition of the cod war. A British warship cruising among them right now is liable to cause an international incident.' He paused. 'Tell you what, though. I'll get on to Peter Inge right away. He should be able to help.'

'Chief of the General Staff of the Army?'

'That's the chap. Just the ticket, I should think.'

'But the Army, Julian?'

'You're forgetting the SBS. They're under Army control, remember? Perfect for what you want. Undercover work, surveillance, and so on. Leave it with me. I'll get back to you.'

Of course, thought the Home Secretary as he replaced the receiver. The SBS. That wonderful, more or less secret unit. Absolutely perfect. If anybody could sniff out the whereabouts of his daughter – assuming she was at sea at all, and if she were not then the chances of finding her without paying a ransom had to be virtually nil – it was the SBS.

Major Zaki Fernandez had personally taken control of Operation Bosom – so named by himself because its aim was to bust a British drug-smuggling ring thought to be running hashish by boat out of Brest. Bust and Brest. Operation Bosom. He was rather pleased with his code-name. Brest, a port on the most westerly tip of France, was the closest area to La Coruña, where an SBS Offshore Patrol Gunboat was stationed. Christened the *Gremlin*, the boat was the pride and joy of Major Fernandez's little fleet. Twenty-six metres long and as sleek as a dolphin, while to all appearances a private yacht, the *Gremlin* had a reinforced, specially designed hull which enabled her to achieve a speed fast enough to overhaul anything but a Riva-type speedboat. She was equipped with a prow-mounted, retractable 9mm L34A1 Sterling sub-machine-gun. When not needed the gun was housed in an electrically operated compartment below a section of deck, undetectable to the untrained eye as a hatch which slid aside at the touch of a button to allow the Sterling to be put into action. Also – and this was a complete innovation as far as any marine or navy boats were concerned – two submersibles – miniature, two-man submarines, their bodies forged of the lightest of space-age metals – sat side by side like torpedoes in special housings below the water-line, on either side of the nestling machine-gun in the very prow of the Patrol Gunboat. They were especially adapted versions of the more usual Vickers Pisces III, battery-operated submersibles; their housings worked like airlocks, they could be flooded when their crew was aboard, and special portholes opened to enable them to be launched. All other boats equipped with submersibles carried them on their decks and they had to be, somewhat clumsily, lowered over the stern.

Major Fernandez was justifiably proud of his disguised gunboat. It was manned by a team of SBS operatives from the Royal Marine Commandos who had been working undercover for several weeks, dressed in the civvies of the typical private yacht owner and guests or in crew

whites. Operation Bosom was about to come
to its conclusion. On the very afternoon of the
kidnapping of Carolyn Parker-Reed the *Gremlin* was all set to arrest a Guernsey-registered
private yacht which had been making frequent
trips between the UK and France, and whose
owner and crew, Fernandez was now certain,
were smuggling drugs in a big way. The major
was fairly confident that there would be a massive
load of hashish aboard – possibly as much as a
thousand kilos.

It was therefore with extreme irritation, just as
he was closing in on his quarry as she moved out
of French territorial waters, that he received orders
from Colonel Sir Peter Inge to abort the mission, set
the *Gremlin* full speed ahead to La Coruña and get
himself by helicopter to the *Mirabelle*.

With great interest, two and a half hours later,
El Asesino observed a Wessex Mk 3 helicopter
descend on to the landing pad of the *Mirabelle*.
The yacht, though big, had only space enough
on her decks for one chopper; the tender helicopter had taken off to park temporarily at La
Coruña airport in order to make room for the
Wessex.

Somebody important was getting into the act,
mused Arsenio as, through his binoculars, he
watched Fernandez descend from the helicopter.
The major was dressed in cream slacks and a white,
open-necked shirt, but something about his bearing

suggested authority, even though he appeared as little more than ant-sized at that distance. Had he not been so far away, Arsenio would surely have recognized him.

As soon as he had been put completely in the picture, Fernandez put a question nobody had thought of to the princes.

'Bubbles?' he asked. 'Did either of you see any bubbles?'

'Not me,' replied the boy who was second in line to succeed to the throne of England.

Neither had Harry, and this, together with the fact that there had been no other boat close by at the time of Carolyn's disappearance, led the major to a wrong conclusion.

'It has to be a submarine,' he said to Parker-Reed. 'She must have been dragged into a sub. There were no bubbles, ergo no frogmen or scuba divers. But one or two men with large lung capacities could go through the airlock of a sub and haul the girl inside within a couple of minutes. A sub it has to be.'

'That seems utterly incredible,' observed the Home Secretary.

'But she's gone. And she's alive. You tell me, sir. If they were, as it seems, really after the Princess of Wales, they would have gone to incredible extremes, would they not?'

'I hate to say this . . . it really hurts me. But we've no proof that she *is* alive, Stephen,' pointed out Travers Bonnington. 'We had a call from a woman, that's all.'

'She's alive,' said Parker-Reed, not even daring to consider the alternative. 'A hoax call is out of the question. Nobody knew of Carolyn's apparent death except for people aboard this boat and my personal secretary.'

'I agree,' said Fernandez. 'From all you've told me she was a very fit young woman and a powerful swimmer. She didn't drown and she was not eaten by sharks. Half the crew went in after her, as did the princess herself. They would have been attacked were there sharks about. There would have been blood. She's been kidnapped all right.' Shaking his head and looking out to sea, where the sky was starting to turn orange at the horizon as the sun began to set, he added, 'They *must* have used a sub.'

The phone rang. It was Kirsty. She would speak to no one but the Home Secretary.

'You should leave. This evening,' she told him. 'Return to England and start to organise the money. Used, untraceable fifty-pound notes. We shall want them delivered in batches of one million pounds. I shall let you know tomorrow when and how for the first million.'

'All right,' said Parker-Reed, lips set in a tight, thin line. 'But I have no proof that Carolyn is alive and well. I have to talk to her. I'm not handing over millions of pounds until I've talked to her.'

'She's not with me. I can't do that.'

'I want to talk to her tomorrow morning,' he insisted firmly. 'I shall be in my London office.' He gave Kirsty the number of his private line.

'I'll see what I can do,' said Kirsty, from the Barcelona exchange.

'What time will she call?'

'I don't know.'

The line went dead.

'I'd have the police set about putting a trace on your London phone right away, sir, if I were you,' said Fernandez, glancing at the stateroom telephone. 'Out here, at sea, poses a certain amount of problems.'

'Yes. Of course. I'll call New Scotland Yard right away. Do you mind, Travers?'

The American looked stunned by this second polite request to use his phone from a man whose daughter had been kidnapped from the *Mirabelle*. 'For Christ's *sake*!' he exploded.

As the sun, a huge ball of fire, began to sink below the horizon, the far-distant fishing boats appeared as a coal-black collection of miniature toys against a brilliant-orange background. Watching the sunset, but his agile mind on other, equally dramatic things, Fernandez suddenly thought of something.

'Those drifters,' he asked Bonnington. 'Were they that far away this morning, when this happened?'

'No. They were much closer, now you come to

mention it,' the American told him. 'About half as far. And one was much nearer to us than the rest, as I recall.'

'Was it now? That could be interesting.'

'Hell, they're just poor fishermen. In any case it was far too far away to swim to. Anyway, someone would have spotted the movement for sure.'

'Probably, yes. Well, we'll just check them out tomorrow morning, in any case. When my *Gremlin* gets here.'

'Your *what*?'

'My Patrol Gunboat. She's heading down from France right now.'

As he said this the thought occurred to Fernandez that scuba divers need not necessarily leave a trail of bubbles. He had forgotten about the specially designed oxygen tanks which retained carbon dioxide. They were available to armed forces personnel only – but the kidnappers might somehow have got hold of some. In any case, an astute man who wanted to cover his tracks might well collect those bubbles in something. A plastic bag, for example. Which would make the task of getting his victim into a submarine that much easier. Or even into a not too far distant fishing boat.

13

Scared, bored, utterly miserable, Carolyn awoke stiff and cramped after a fitful night's sleep. Arsenio had tried to make her as comfortable as possible, rustling up some old fishing nets to put under her blanket, and she had been offered food and drink the evening before. He had even let her out of her prison to use the boat's primitive toilet facilities. But she had not been able to eat – her nervous stomach would not allow it; she had only managed to slake her thirst. During the night the nets kept bunching into uncomfortable lumps beneath her, and when she did snatch moments of sleep they were disturbed by awful dreams.

Now, with the drifter rolling in an increasing swell, she felt queasy again – a condition which was not helped by the smell of her stale vomit which filtered through the fishy stink of the hold.

The hatch above her head opened and she was momentarily blinded by the bright light which flooded in. It was 9 a.m., but as far as she was concerned it might have been afternoon. Felix

Springer let himself down, then closed the hatch almost snug so that there was just enough light slipping through to see by. He had been sent down on a mission which Arsenio personally had little stomach for. He had with him the portable telephone, and a note whose contents Carolyn was to read to Kirsty in Barcelona and which Kirsty was to tape-record. Arsenio needed Carolyn to sound terrified when she read the note – enough to be sobbing uncontrollably. That way her father, when he heard the recording over his London telephone, might be persuaded to come up with the ransom without any attempts at playing for time.

'Well, my pretty one,' said Springer, ogling Carolyn in the dim light. 'You are having the most nicest tits, is this not so?' Rape was not what El Asesino had had in mind when he told the German to 'scare the shit out of her, but don't actually do her any physical damage'. Springer had other ideas. The chick was their prisoner, she was fair game.

Carolyn's bright-blue eyes went very wide. She had sat up as Springer came into the hold, and now she stood and backed away from him, folding her arms protectively over the thin, pale-green sweater which had been meant for the Princess of Wales. 'What do you . . . you want?' she stuttered. 'You just stay away from me, you hear? Keep *away*.'

'*Nein*. I want to see your tits. Is OK, no?'

She staggered as the boat rolled, and then he

was on her, clamping her wrists together behind her back in a huge, meaty hand, forcing her on to her knees on the blanket and fishing nets, ripping her sweater up to her shoulders, greedily fumbling her breasts.

Gasping, she fought to free her hands, but he was a powerful man, and she had no chance. Instead, she leant into him and sank her teeth into his black-T-shirted shoulder. He grunted, stopped mauling her breasts, and shoved her face off him.

'So – you are wanting to play games, is it?' He grinned, crinkling a scar in his artificially bronzed cheek. 'Then, OK, is good. We play games. I fuck you, girl. OK?'

His hand clamped over her mouth, he forced her on to her back and fell on top of her, his solid fifteen-stone weight pressing her into the nets, squashing her as he unzipped her jeans and ripped them down and off one leg, then did the same with the bikini bottom. As he released her mouth to fumble undone his own jeans she let rip a piercing scream which penetrated the entire boat.

Within seconds, as Springer handled himself out and prepared to enter her, the hatch was dragged fully open and the hold flooded with light.

'Cut it *out*, Felix,' said Arsenio, coldly. 'That's not what I . . .'

Springer looked over his shoulder and up. 'But you told me to . . .' he cut in, and was himself interrupted.

'I didn't tell you to rape her, lunkhead. Get *off* her.'

But the German was far gone in his lust. He was determined to have his way. 'You *get* me off her,' he growled, at the same time pulling down his jeans enough to present Arsenio with a view of his huge, hairy buttocks. He forced Carolyn's wildly kicking legs wide.

Arsenio sighed. He needed this like he needed the proverbial head hole. He pulled out the Smith & Wesson from its holster beneath his shirt.

'*Felix*,' he shouted, crouching down and pointing the gun into the hold. The sound of the safety-catch clicking off was sharp and unnaturally loud in the echoing emptiness.

The German recognized that noise. He turned his head once more, eyes blazing.

'I'll use it. You know I will. Now turn it *in*.'

Rolling off Carolyn, Springer pulled up his jeans. 'OK. OK,' he muttered, anger seething within him to override his lust. 'But still I cannot see why . . .' His eyes were raking the young woman's nakedness as she struggled to cover herself.

'Get on with it. What you're supposed to be doing, for Christ's sake. I'll be watching. I'll put some lead in your arse if you try that again.' Closing the hatch three-quarters of the way, Arsenio remained above it, with his gun ready, observing.

'When I am getting my chance,' muttered the

frustrated German to Carolyn, 'I shall be doing it to you real good. In every sort of way. You will see. Just you wait.'

She was sitting up, panting, warily staring at him. 'What, what is it you're supposed to be doing to me?' she whispered. She glanced up at Arsenio. 'What's he *supposed* to be doing to me, for God's sake?'

His face stony, Arsenio merely shrugged. He was not enjoying this one little bit.

Springer pulled a large penknife from the back pocket of his jeans. He opened it. The blade, kept lovingly sharp, gleamed. Grabbing Carolyn's hand, he forced it flat on to the wooden hull, doubling her over in the process. 'I have to cut off a finger. To send to your papa,' he hissed.

'*Noooo*,' Carolyn wailed. 'No! Please, *please*.' Her shoulders began heaving, she started to blubber.

'But that is for the next time. When he does not pay us quickly enough. This time is just some hair.' Grabbing hold of her short, blonde hair, he twisted a bunch of it viciously and hacked it off close to the roots. Then, with his horrified victim quaking with fright and moaning and blubbering, he picked up the portable telephone from where he had left it before his attempted rape, and punched the keys. When he was through to Kirsty, he pulled a sheet of paper from his pocket and thrust it in front of Carolyn's tear-filled eyes. 'Read,' he said.

'Dry the eyes and read. Now. Or the finger, it does come off.'

In Barcelona, Kirsty pressed the microphone of a sensitive tape recorder tight on the telephone receiver.

Considering it had been taped over a telephone line, then the tape played over another line, Carolyn's voice was remarkably clear – and her acute distress most painfully obvious.

'Hello, Papa, it's me, Carolyn,' she said between great sobs. 'I'm all right. I don't know where I am. I'm in a house somewhere. I'm being kept locked up in the dark and I am being treated quite badly, but I have been fed. It's horrible. They have cut off some of my hair and they have told me that they mean to cut . . .' – here she broke down, unable to do anything else but blubber for several seconds – 'to, to cut other *bits* off me, starting with, with . . . a *finger* and to send them to you if you don't pay what they are asking. Oh, Papa, it's quite, quite ghastly. Do please pay them and get me out of here as soon as you can.'

That was the end of the pathetic message. The Home Secretary had to make a supreme effort to pull himself together in order to pay attention to what Kirsty was now telling him.

'Do you have the first million?' she asked him.

'How can you treat her like that? Scare her like

that? I *am* going to pay you,' said Parker-Reed, failing to control the shake in his voice.

'I'm just a go-between,' Kirsty told him. She was – perhaps unjustifiably – convinced that her lover would let no real harm come to the girl, that the words he had put into her mouth were merely bluff. 'What about the money?'

'I'm not the bloody Bank of England.'

'So you really want a grisly little jet-service parcel? They're prepared to lop off her pinkie at any moment.' Again, El Asesino's words.

'Christ. I'm organizing the money. It'll be together late this afternoon. Don't hurt her, for pity's sake.'

'All right. I'll call you at five.' The line went dead. Distraught, the Home Secretary stared at it for long, silent, fear-filled seconds. Then he punched buttons and got through directly to the governor of Lloyd's Bank, a personal friend of his who was sorting out the money angle.

As for trying to locate Carolyn, everything humanly possible had been put into operation. Interpol were aware of the situation, and the Spanish Guardia Civil were already doing what they could in and around Barcelona. There was a police technician working in Parker-Reed's secretary's office, trying to trace the kidnappers' calls, and even now he was homing in, thanks to the miracle of computerized technology, on the Barcelona telephone exchange which Kirsty had used earlier. And, down in the south of the Bay of Biscay – which was beginning to cut up rough – the *Gremlin* had just arrived at the snatch scene and was making fast to the *Mirabelle*.

As soon as Captain Douglas Derby – a muscular man dressed in white cut-off jeans and a blue-denim shirt, a highly experienced officer whom Fernandez would trust with his life – was aboard the *Mirabelle*, the SBS major explained the situation to him, and how he wanted it handled.

'. . . and so, we keep our cover as a private yacht, OK?' he finished. 'Except that once we're among the drifters and looking around, the fisherman are going to assume we're fishery inspectors and possibly start getting a bit hostile. Well, let them. Let's go.'

When they were both on the *Gremlin* and she cast off, the first thing Fernandez ordered was the two submersibles manned and launched to search the seabed for a possible submarine. Then he set a leisurely course towards the fishing boats, all of which had in the past hour, as if they were one fleet and not a whole collection of independent operators, started their engines and begun to move back towards the *Mirabelle*, because they had drifted to the edge of the fishing ground. Even so, the nearest boat – no longer *La Señorita Juanita*, which had got in among the thick of them – was still about five kilometres distant.

The SBS Patrol Gunboat reached the motley

fleet in twenty minutes. Once there, her engines were cut so that she was moving no faster than a rowing boat. The drifters were in many cases quite close together as far as their sides were concerned, with no more than fifty metres separating them. But great distances were between the stern of one ragged line and the prow of the second so that they did not interfere with one another's nets.

There were only two lines, each of some thirty ships. The *Gremlin* crept among them, drawing – as Fernandez had anticipated – hollered insults and shouts of protest in four languages, one of which was Irish Gaelic. Every fisherman believed that here was a boat from one Ministry of Fisheries or another poking its unwelcome nose in.

Every fisherman except for the crew of *La Señorita Juanita*. For Arsenio, watchful as ever, had just been able to make out that the sleek-looking boat that now moved between them had first visited the *Mirabelle*. He had been expecting something like this – and he was ready for it. The kidnappers got down to some unaccustomed work.

The names, registration numbers and port of origin of each boat were being noted by the SBS men – not always an easy task since the sea was now quite heavy and the bows of the boats were dipping and rolling, much of the time immersed in waves. This obvious activity thoroughly convinced the fishermen that the stranger was a ministry boat, and the insults kept flying to be snatched away on the wind. Each name and number was checked out via computer links by the radio operator. It was going to be a lengthy task.

When, some half an hour after the job had begun, the *Gremlin* drew level with *La Señorita Juanita*, some twenty metres leeward of her, Arsenio and his men were busy winching the nets and clearing them of a plenteous haul of striped tunny. Arsenio shouted rich epithets across the rough intervening sea at them in Spanish, '*Me cago en la leche de su puta madre*' – I shit in the milk of your whore of a mother – being one of the choicest. Pepe Pomares was at the wheel, staring blankly ahead, not daring – though he guessed that this was some sort of a police boat looking for the girl – to make the slightest sign of distress.

Down in the hold, Carolyn, having eaten a little half an hour before and then vomited it all up, was suffering a new torture. For there was only one place for freshly caught, living fish to be thrown when they were cleared from the nets: down with her. One by one the big, striped tunny, some of them larger than her thigh and weighing several kilos, were flung down through the open hatch – which she had been warned on pain of death not to try to climb up through – to thump and crash in front of her. They came thick and fast, for Arsenio and the other three were putting on a convincing act for the benefit of the *Gremlin*, aboard which Pomares' registration was at that moment being checked through the competent Spanish authorities.

Fish were writhing and leaping around on the deck, in their death throes, more and more of them, every so often one of them reaching where Carolyn was cowering against a bulkhead, flopping pathetically over her bare feet. It was hot down there, but she was shivering at the grim sight. If she got out of her predicament alive, she had decided, she would never eat another fish again.

La Señorita Juanita checked out perfectly OK. Fernandez thought the crew were rather short-handed, but that was hardly of any importance – there were probably some sick men ashore.

The *Gremlin* moved on, cutting through waves that piled over her elegant prow and broke over the deck to pour back down over the sides.

Every drifter, as Fernandez had feared, was the genuine article. There was no criminal intruder in among them. The news from the submersibles was negative, too. No submarine lurked anywhere in the vicinity. But they were continuing to do a thorough radar scan of the seabed in the hope that a sub might be discovered. Of course, it would not be, the major brooded. They might just as well have stayed at Brest and made their very important arrest. It might well be too late to pull the drug smugglers in when he got back; that last assignment was so huge it was probably their last one for a while. And then they would most likely completely change tactics, making the crucial part of the SBS investigation worthless. Such is life, he thought. A bitch – then you die.

He ordered the *Gremlin* to about turn and head back through the fishing boats.

Trouble was brewing – trouble that Arsenio could never have anticipated. For the illegal length of Pomares' nets – something of which Arsenio was blissfully unaware – had been spotted by a keen eye aboard a nearby Irish drifter.

'Those bastards are overfishing,' growled one of the crew. 'Those Spanish buggers over to port. *La Senoreeta Jewaneeta.*'

The captain watched the activity aboard Pomares' boat for a minute or so, eyes, as green as his country, steely. ''Tis so much for the fookin' ministry boat. Under their soddin' noses and they don't see a thing, they don't.'

The *Gremlin* was now five hundred metres past them on its way back to the *Mirabelle*. As he had done on his passage through, the navigator was careful, when he had to cross nets, to pass right between the centre of two widely spaced floats, where his hull could not do any damage to the net.

The captain of the Irish boat, the *Dancing Leprechaun*, was a hard-drinking, hard-headed, quarrelsome man from Galway. When he got angry it seethed through him, uncontrollable.

'Overfishin', is it?' he grumbled. 'Oi'll show the fookin' bastards, so I will.'

Coaxing his engines to full throttle, he turned the boat's nose towards the side of *La Señorita Juanita* and bore down on her. The *Dancing Leprechaun* hit Pomares' boat plumb amidships, rising with a big wave just before the collision, crashing down into her with a rending, splintering racket, throwing over every man on both drifters, except those at the wheels.

In the hold of the Spanish boat, Carolyn went flying, to fall over and roll among the heap of dying fish, screaming dementedly.

Hantash, bleeding from a deep cut in his cheek where it had caught the ship's rail as he was flung over, was first to his feet, swearing. The Irish boat, he saw, was backing off to have another go. He dragged his Czechoslovakian CZ75 9mm handgun from his shoulder holster and pointed it in two hands at the bridge of the *Dancing Leprechaun*.

'Back off, you stupid bastards,' he yelled, as the Irishman started his boat at them again.

'Guns, is it? You wouldn't dare, boyo,' growled the captain, mainly to himself. He aimed the prow of his boat amidships again, at the point where *La Señorita Juanita* was badly splintered.

Dare, Hantash certainly would. Aiming carefully, he put a bullet through the Irishman's temple. The captain was dead even before his boat rammed the Spanish drifter for the second time.

Daylight was seeping through into the hold, and with the second collision the gash in the side of the vessel opened wider. Carolyn's nightmare was worsening – she had just managed to drag herself to her feet, with tunny flopping around her ankles, when she was knocked over again. She was hysterical, her screams intensified, and they were carried on the wind as far as the *Gremlin*.

A split second after the crunch of wood on wood reached his ears, Fernandez had assessed the situation behind him, and his craft was making a sweeping turn in the sea, buffeted badly by the waves as she did so. Quarrels between fishermen were hardly his business, but he was not about to sit tight and let one boat try to sink another. Then came the scream – unquestionably a woman's scream. As the SBS boat straightened out and picked up speed, there was the sound of a gunshot, followed by another crunch – and the screaming got rapidly louder.

It was *her* – she was there aboard one of the two clashing boats, of that the major was certain. Fishermen did not take their womenfolk to sea. As the *Gremlin* closed in fast on *La Señorita Juanita* her 9mm Sterling machine-gun was sliding up from within the prow, coincidentally manned by the same SBS Sergeant Stride who had been on watch on the Thames the evening Arsenio had attacked the House of Lords. He was sitting on the little metal seat which was one of the gun's accessories, rising with it, ready for action.

'Jesus *Christ*!' breathed Arsenio as the gunboat

closed in on them. It was too late to stop the stupid bitch from screaming now. Hantash had overreacted, and there was a dead man at the helm of the Irish boat, which, rammed against *La Señorita Juanita*, was shoving her sideways. It was too late for anything – except for naked aggression.

'Nobody moves,' Fernandez called through his battery-operated loudhailer when the *Gremlin* was almost on the drifter and slowing down. 'Freeze on board there.' To emphasize his words, he ordered Stride to put a burst of the Sterling over the drifter's bridge.

But somebody did move – and faster than the major could have dreamed in his worst nightmare. El Asesino was not giving up without a fight. Death was preferable to going back to jail. He had set out on this operation equipped for just such an emergency. In a bag close to the bridge he had a cluster of deadly weapons – 30mm hand-grenades. Dropping to his hands and knees on the deck, he crawled, beneath the protection of the high side of the boat, to the bag. With the *Gremlin* only metres away, he took three grenades from the bag, pulled the pins from all of them in quick succession, waited five seconds, rose up on his knees and, with Stride swinging the nose of the Sterling to get a bead on him, lobbed them one after the other on to the deck of the SBS boat.

Stride got his priorities right, but it failed to save

him, or his ship. He left his post at the machine-gun to dive on a grenade which had fallen near him, intending to sling it over the side. It went off in his hand, blowing him to pieces. Fernandez was standing by the rail, waiting to board *La Señorita Juanita*. The power of the blast threw him overboard with several pieces of shrapnel embedded in his back – and so saved his life.

For, while grenade number two bounced off the keel of the *Gremlin* and went off harmlessly in the sea, number three went clean through an open hatch and fell into the engine room, where it exploded near the fuel tanks.

The pride and joy of the small fleet of SBS Patrol Gunboats went up like a bomb, with a great rumbling roar and a massive, all-engulfing belch of flame and black smoke, everyone aboard dying with her. Within seconds what was left of her was gone without a trace, sinking down, with the blasted bodies, to the bottom of the Bay of Biscay.

The blast of heat from the explosion, hotter than the hottest sirocco, scorched over *La Señorita Juanita* and was immediately tugged away in the wind.

'Get out of here,' Arsenio screamed to Pomares on the bridge. 'Malpica as fast as she will go.'

With Pomares swinging the boat around and starting to bring her up to her maximum speed of twelve knots, Arsenio hacked through the main line of the net. To Pomares' dismay, the two kilometres of his fishing net which had not been hauled in — one and a half kilometres of them illegal and the cause of the Irish skipper's fury and the subsequent mayhem and destruction — were left behind.

On board the *Mirabelle*, Diana and the boys having long since departed, Travers Bonnington was reading a book by the side of his pool when the distant sound of a shot from the direction of the fishing boats alerted him to trouble. His binoculars were trained on the *Gremlin* at the moment she went up. Shaken, he ordered his crew to weigh anchor and take his yacht as quickly as possible to the scene.

Fernandez, blood seeping in several places through the back of his soaked shirt and slacks, was taken aboard the *Dancing Leprechaun*. In pain, not seriously injured but losing a great deal of blood, he gazed in profound shock at the place in the heavy sea where his craft had disappeared; there was nothing left of it but a big patch of black oil in the wave troughs. His beloved boat, its good Captain Douglas Derby, and its crew of highly trained Royal Marine commandos, had all vanished without trace, for ever. It was Arsenio, without a shadow of a doubt. He thought he remembered that face, even with the beard. Not for nothing was the man known as the Assassin.

The major's vision was beginning to blur as his

gaze fell on the fleeing *Señorita Juanita*. His last thought before he collapsed to the deck of the Irish drifter, on the point of passing out, was that he had got El Asesino once before, and would get him again. He would not rest until he had the bastard.

'I can't raise *Gremlin*,' observed Corporal Tweedy, at the pilot's console near the ocean floor in the submersible *Shark*. 'Not a dicky-bird.'

'Odd,' said his companion, another corporal, John Bright. 'Maybe we've gone on the blink?'

'I'll try and raise *Squid*.' He was referring to the other specially adapted Vickers Pisces III submersible, scouring the seabed with them.

Tweedy had no trouble at all getting through to *Squid* on their Marconi Modular sub-to-sub system. *Squid*, hardly surprisingly, could not raise their mother ship either.

'Something's up,' said Corporal Bright. 'We'd better surface.'

'Without orders?'

'So how're we gonna get orders, berk? We could stay down here waiting for them until we run out of oxygen.'

Meanwhile, as the *Mirabelle* closed in on the fleet of fishing boats, through his binoculars Bonnington saw that in the thick of them, in the region where the *Gremlin* had blown up, someone was waving a shirt. He told his captain to head for that boat. Neither of them paid much attention to the Spanish drifter which had passed them, heading south.

By the time Bonnington's yacht reached the *Dancing Leprechaun*, one of the Irishmen had roughly patched up Fernandez, who was coming round. The American went aboard to find the skipper, a hole through his head, stretched out on the deck.

'What the hell happened here?' he asked.

Three men tried to gabble the story at once. Bonnington managed to shut two of them up, then got the information from the one who had seen to Fernandez's wounds.

'He's got shrapnel embedded all over his back,' said the Irishman as Fernandez pushed himself up with a groan.

'*Shrapnel?*' echoed Bonnington. 'How's that possible?'

'Grenade,' said the major weakly. 'The son of a bitch lobbed grenades at us. One must have rolled down into the engine room for *Gremlin* to go up like that.' He shook his head, utterly miserable. 'Those poor, poor bastards. Their families. God.'

'What son of a bitch?' asked the American.

'Arsenio. That terrorist character. It was him, I know it was, the evil bastard. I recognized him. I know him. It was me who arrested him after he bombed the House of Lords.'

Bonnington's lean jaw dropped. 'Christ, man! Then Carolyn's on that boat.' His grey eyes swept the sea. 'Which one is it?'

143

'It's taken off. Most likely making a run for harbour. *La Señorita Juanita*, out of Malpica.'

'Then we've gotta get after them. *Carolyn's* on board.'

'And what are you going to do when you catch them up? They're armed and homicidal. I don't know what other weapons they have with them – they may even have the capacity to hole your ship.'

'Jesus.'

'If you'll get me aboard your yacht, I'll see what help I can bring out here. But it'll have to be fast or we're going to lose them.' He grimaced. 'And I'll need a doctor. Can your chopper fly one to me?'

'I can do better than that. There's a doctor aboard. I wasn't taking the risk of being without one with the Princess of Wales and her kids as guests.'

As Fernandez was being assisted into the *Mirabelle's* speedboat to cross the few metres of sea between the Irish boat and her, he spotted the submersibles *Shark* and *Squid*, on the surface, converging on them from two different directions, and being tossed around violently.

'My little subs,' he said. 'I'd forgotten about them. I'll get the swine yet.'

'They'll have to take it easy. Don't lose sight of the fact that they've got the daughter of the Home Secretary.'

'You're right. They'll do whatever they can without risking her life.'

The submersibles were not designed to ride the surface of a rough sea. As they drew alongside the speedboat, Tweedy was the only man to appear through a hatch. Hanging on the curved metal conning tower of the *Shark*, on the concave top which served as a deck, the corporal was receiving a thorough soaking as he was informed what had happened and what their course of action was to be. The *Shark* was being tossed around like a twig in white water.

When Tweedy descended into the cramped interior of the submersible with its curved walls covered in gauges and dials, he was in grim mood indeed. Sixteen good men, friends and colleagues of his, had gone down with the *Gremlin*, and Tweedy was out for blood. When he passed the news on to Bright, and then radioed it to the *Squid*, three more men were out for revenge. The submersibles dived down into the calm beneath them, and set off after *La Señorita Juanita*.

Fifteen minutes later, Arsenio was presented with yet another totally unexpected and alarming development when, twenty metres on either side of him, travelling parallel and at exactly the same speed as the fishing boat, two little six-metre-long submarines popped to the surface. They were going with the waves now, bouncing up and down but not rolling. A man climbed up through a hatch on each of them. Men bearing Armalite rifles with M203 grenade launchers. One of them – Corporal Bright – also held a loudhailer.

'You are under arrest,' called Bright. 'Throw your arms and ammunition over the side and accompany us to the nearest port.'

Arsenio stared coldly at him. You've got to be kidding, boy, he thought. 'Get Carolyn up here,' he calmly told Hantash.

'Surrender, or we open fire,' came Bright's amplified voice.

Arsenio cupped his big hands. 'We have a girl aboard,' he shouted. 'Our prisoner. The daughter of your Home Secretary. You must know about her, or you wouldn't be here.'

'Release her into our custody,' said Bright.

'Balls.'

Carolyn, weepy, appeared on deck. Hantash had her tightly gripped above the elbow. Being deliberately rough with her, he shoved her to the ship's rail. 'Either you vanish, or she gets hurt,' menaced Arsenio.

'You can't win. You'll shortly have more than us to cope with,' replied Bright. 'Give up now. Don't be a fool.'

The SBS corporal watched, dismayed, as Felix Springer closed in on Carolyn, produced a knife, and seized the struggling girl's right forearm just above the wrist. He forced it flat down on the top

146

of the boat's side, her hand hanging over its edge,
over the water.

'I'm going to count to ten,' shouted Arsenio. 'If
you've not vanished by the time I reach it, her
finger comes off. Then you get another ten, and
it's another finger. And so on, until you get the
message. One, two, three . . .' He was counting
quickly.

'Why, you fucking *bastard*,' muttered Bright.
Hurriedly, as Arsenio reached seven, he made a
hand signal to the *Squid*.

It was with considerable relief that El Asesino
watched the commandos disappear down into their
conning towers, the hatches close and the subs
dive. He would, he realized, have been forced
to carry out his threat. It would only have been
the one finger, of course. After that they would
have gone, all right. But it would have been
a particularly nasty thing to have inflicted on
an innocent girl. A rather lovely innocent girl,
at that.

His eyes searched the rough surface of the sea.
They were down there, of course. *La Señorita
Juanita* would be a blip on their radar screens.
They would follow them all the way in to Malpica
harbour.

He sighed. He would have to deal with that
problem when they arrived. This kidnap business
was proving to be far trickier than he had anticipated. Hantash had shot dead an Irish skipper and

he himself had blown up what he now realized had
been an SBS Patrol Gunboat.

The entire world and his dog would be trying to
track him down.

14

There was very little activity in Malpica harbour when *La Señorita Juanita* chugged in. As he watched the spreading furrows in the calm water behind her, looking for signs of the submersibles, Arsenio ordered Pomares not to put his ship in her customary place alongside the outer harbour wall, but to take her as near the town side of the harbour as possible and back her into the wall, keeping her engines running so that her helm stayed tight against the concrete.

'We're going into a port,' said Corporal Tweedy over the radio to the following *Squid*. Above him, the hulls of moored boats were slipping by. Afternoon sunlight was penetrating the slightly murky waters to pick out the torpedo-shaped submersibles as, one in front of the other, they slid further into Malpica harbour. Arsenio's eyes narrowed.

'We can't do anything down here,' responded the pilot of the *Squid*. 'We should surface.'

In the hold of the drifter, Carolyn was in yet more trouble. The waves which had been smashing over the drifter had been throwing water constantly through the gash in the boat's side, and Carolyn was up to her calves in it. The last of the tunny had been saved at almost their final gasp as the first inches of sea water splashed in, and they were swimming around her and knocking into her legs, though she could not see them because the hatch was closed fast. All this had not happened to her, she told herself; it was not happening. She was becoming convinced that she was going out of her mind.

As the helm of *La Señorita Juanita* bumped into the harbour wall, some fifty metres from it the *Shark* and the *Squid* surfaced. Hantash and Springer were already hauling Carolyn from the hold and Kasar had leapt ashore. Arsenio was ready for the submersibles. He did not have a launcher, but he was certainly capable of hurling a grenade accurately over that distance. He pulled the pin and chucked one, then sent another after it for good measure. The first clanged against the hull of the *Shark* and bounced off, the second splashed into the water behind it, halfway between its tail and the *Squid*'s nose.

The grenades went off within two seconds of one another. There were two water-muffled *whumphs*, followed by great fountains of water spurting five or six metres into the air. Inside the submersibles, the sound of pieces of shrapnel clanging against the hulls came at the same time as the shock waves racing through the water hit them. The subs were rocked so violently that Tweedy, who had been standing and opening the hatch above him, was flung sideways and knocked unconscious as his head hit a protruding metal gauge.

Arsenio and the others, dragging Carolyn between them, had disembarked and were running from the harbour when the grenades went off. It was the hour of the siesta, and there were few people about, but those that were there stopped and stared in amazement at the four fisherman and the barefoot girl rushing from the harbour, whose waters were still hitting the walls in waves as a result of the two massive explosions. Then every one of them hurried into the harbour to see what had happened to disturb the peace of their normally uneventful town.

As the frantic bobbing of the *Shark* eased off, Bright caught a glimpse through one of the three portholes of the fleeing men and their hostage, reaching the promenade, dashing across it and disappearing down a side-street. The only chance he had of catching them was to beach the submersible. As Tweedy, groaning, picked himself off the deck, half of his face coated in blood, Bright put the *Shark* on full thrust and shot towards the forefront of the harbour. The men in the *Squid*, getting the idea, went after them.

The handful of onlookers had never seen anything like it. First, explosions, then great spouts of water. Armed fishermen dragging a girl along with them. A pair of strange-looking, small submarines shooting through the harbour, crunching on to its gently sloping, littered, muddy beach. Three men in trainers, denim shorts and T-shirts, armed with sub-machine-guns, clambering from the subs, leaping into the shallow water and rushing through it and up on to the promenade. A fourth, with a blood-soaked face, dragging himself groggily through a hatch.

It had to be that a movie was being shot – except that there were no cameras, no director and no film crew.

The SBS commandos, despite their speedy reaction, were too far behind Arsenio's band to have much of a chance of catching them. The kidnappers had crammed Carolyn into the hired Panda – still standing outside the Pomares' house – had piled in all around her and were away, Arsenio at the wheel, tearing through the streets of Malpica, by the time the first of the commandos turned the corner of the little row of fishermen's cottages to see not a soul, or a moving car, in the road.

Tweedy, meanwhile, had recovered sufficiently to carry out one, quite futile, operation. Spotting movement aboard *La Señorita Juanita*, carrying his sub-machine-gun at the ready, he cautiously crept up on the drifter to leap aboard and menace Pomares with death if he did not lie down flat on his deck with his arms above his head.

Pomares understood not a word that the commando flung at him, but the gun spoke all languages. Swearing under his breath, the tough old fisherman did as Tweedy – already realizing that he was probably making a mistake – asked him.

15

'I need an operations centre. There's a fully
equipped SBS boat setting out from Portsmouth
right now, but she won't arrive for at least
twenty-four hours.' Major Fernandez, shirtless,
his torso swathed in clean white bandages, was
sipping coffee in the stateroom of the *Mirabelle*
with Travers Bonnington as he spoke.

'You need a hospital. My doctor's got out as
much of the shrapnel as he can. But you know
damn well there might be pieces buried in deeper.
You need an X-ray urgently. If there's any more
junk inside you it has to be got out before a bit of
it floats into a vital organ.' The American puffed
his Havana. 'And kills you,' he added bluntly.

'I'll have to take a chance on that.' Fernandez
was stirring his already well-stirred coffee, a fierce
expression on his granite face. 'The priority right
now is tracking down Arsenio. Nothing else matters. He wiped out the *Gremlin* and all aboard. He
has the Home Secretary's daughter with him. I'm
going to get him.'

154

'Easier said than done.' Bonnington shrugged. 'It's your life, I guess.' He stood. 'OK – you need an operations room, you've got one. I keep in daily touch with the world's stock markets. Take a look in here.' He led Fernandez into an adjoining cabin. It was fully equipped with the latest in computer technology, including a modem and a laser image scanner, and there were two fax machines. A male secretary worked a ten-hour day in there. 'It's all at your disposal,' said the American. 'This is Gavin, he'll help you in any way you want. How does it suit you?'

Gavin was in his early thirties and good-looking in a male-model sort of way. When he smiled and said hello it was immediately obvious that he was gay. And therefore perhaps doubly efficient, thought Fernandez.

'Good afternoon,' said the major. He looked all around and then back at Bonnington. 'First-class,' he commented. 'All I could possibly want.'

He hardly knew where to start. He was a highly trained fighting machine, a leader of men, most skilled in the tactics of warfare and specifically of anti-criminal operations on water. But at that moment there was a void to fill. His submersibles had taken off an hour and a half earlier after *La Señorita Juanita* and he did not have their damned contact numbers – that was something he left to his radio operator and the poor bastard was at the bottom of the sea.

But there was the Wessex. Of course, the chopper that had lifted him here was still sitting on the deck.

'Raise the helicopter pilot, would you please?' he asked Gavin. 'I'm going aloft.'

'But you're in no fit state to go running around, feller,' said Bonnington. 'You've lost a lot of blood.'

'I've had a steak sandwich and half a bottle of Beaujolais. I'll be OK.'

Recalling that the drifter had been registered at Malpica, Fernandez found the town on the map. Calculating that it lay in more or less the direction that the boat had fled, as soon as he was in the helicopter he told the pilot to set off for the town.

Fifteen minutes later, flying low, he spotted his two submersibles beached at Malpica harbour. And there she was, *La Señorita Juanita*. There was quite a crowd around her on the dockside. There were two Guardia Civil jeeps and an ambulance. His four commandos from the submersibles, he saw, were on board. Hopes rising, he told the pilot to put the Wessex down on the harbour wall across from the fishing boat, as bystanders moved hastily out of the down-draught.

Fernandez had been brought up to speak Spanish and Greek – as well as English – at home, and now the first served him well, for there was utter confusion on board *La Señorita Juanita*. None

156

of his men spoke Spanish, none of the Guardia Civil English. Corporal Bright was attempting the practically impossible job of explaining what he and his fellow commandos were doing there with their Sterling sub-machine-guns and their little submarines and why they had the locally well-known skipper Pepe Pomares lying flat on the deck of his boat. Meanwhile a number of people in the crowd – growing by the second as it seemed all the inhabitants of Malpica were pouring down to the harbour – were shouting and gesticulating wildly as they told the story in their different fashions to the police.

The Guardia Civil also had their machine-guns, as well as sidearms, and all six of them were nervously fingering, though not pointing, the former. It was plain that they had no idea what to do, but when Fernandez clambered on board – the boat had been precariously made fast with a single rope – one of the sergeants was protesting that surely they should arrest these foreigners and cart them off to the local police station.

Pomares was finally being allowed to his feet as Fernandez indentified himself. The SBS major towered over the policemen, his presence and manner commanding. They believed him immediately, and besides, there were the submarines, and now the helicopter, as evidence to back him up. Nevertheless, the sergeant pointed out, these people had no right charging around on Spanish soil with loaded sub-machine-guns, and subjecting the good Pepe Pomares to such violent treatment.

Fernandez speedily sorted it all out by getting the fisherman to tell his story. Long before the major had filled in the gaps, the Spaniards realized exactly what had been going on. The entire province was on alert for any sign of the whereabouts of an important British young lady, and the countryside was being scoured, and subjected to roadblocks, by patrols of both the Guardia Civil and the Guardia Municipal. Spain's Military Intelligence was involved, as were the Special Anti-Terrorist Brigade of the Judicial Police and the National Police's Organized Crime Group. This was a kidnapping of major international importance which had been carried out just outside Spanish territorial waters, so that there was the strong possibility that the victim was even now on Spanish soil.

Carolyn Parker-Reed was indeed on Spanish soil. Not much more than half an hour earlier she had been hustled off *La Señorita Juanita*, and rushed into the village. Perhaps she was *still* in the village. The members of the Guardia Civil were galvanized into action; not only, they had learned, was the important señorita from London not far away, but the poor wife of Pepe Pomares was being held prisoner somewhere too.

At that moment, in the little, rented holiday house on the banks of the Río Allones, Señora Pomares, locked in a dark bedroom whose windows were heavily shuttered and door locked, was listening to the sounds of frenzied activity in the rest of the house. A car had arrived, and there were loud male voices and shouts. There was also a woman, but she hardly spoke.

Carolyn Parker-Reed was slowly coming out of what had been a zombie-like state of shock. Unreality was – she was slowly coming to grips with the fact – reality after all. She had been abducted by the infamous Arsenio while swimming in the Bay of Biscay; she had been imprisoned in the stinking hold of a fishing boat; she had been attacked and almost raped by a brute with a German accent; she had been threatened with having her finger cut off, then made to make a tearful tape-recording for her father; she had had hundreds of huge, living fish thrown down on her; the boat had been holed above the water-line by another; there had been a gunshot; apparently some sort of police launch had ordered her captors to give in and there had been three massive explosions; they had headed off somewhere and been ordered to surrender by a man on one of two miniature submarines – as meanwhile the hold was slowly filling with water; she had been taken on deck and again threatened with having a finger hacked off; they had put into a harbour somewhere, where there had been two more explosions; she had been rushed off the boat, through some narrow streets and shoved into the back of a little car, crushed between two massive men, one of whom was the would-be rapist; and now she had been plonked into a chair and ordered not to move, while her captors were hurriedly changing clothes all around her.

Arsenio's brain was in top gear. The local countryside, he realized, would be crawling with police in next to no time. They did not have much of a start. Four men and a girl were number-one police priority to be hunted down. But now they were five, plus Carolyn – and there was not an inch of room for one more man in the Panda. They needed extra transport – urgently.

The road on which the rented house was situated was little more than a bumpy track alongside the river, the only traffic to pass along it fishermen, botanists, a few adventurous holidaymakers – and that only occasionally.

Pedro Castillo was proud of his twenty-year-old Harley-Davidson motor cycle. He kept it finely tuned, lavished loving attention on it, and cleaned it every week. He would never have brought it down this bumpy track at all had it not been for one simple fact. He had a new girlfriend and had wanted to take her somewhere romantic and out of the way during their extended lunch break from the garage in which he worked and from her mother's haberdashery shop, in the little town of Villaverde, in order to press his sexual attentions on her.

Pedro had failed on this day to achieve the coveted goal, but he had at least made progress and he was feeling fairly pleased with himself as, very slowly and carefully, he negotiated the bumps, ruts and potholes in the narrow lane while taking himself and his girl back to work.

As he approached the kidnappers' rented house, Arsenio came staggering and reeling down the path from the front door, both hands clutched to his heart. As Pedro's bike was almost on him, he collapsed in the track in front of it, writhing and moaning. The young man stopped, dismounted and bent over the stricken figure, to find himself looking into the barrel of a Smith & Wesson 459 as another man, also bearing a handgun, ran out of the house.

Within minutes, Pedro and his girlfriend were tightly bound hand and foot, and gagged, and locked up in the dark with Señora Pomares.

Arsenio seldom went anywhere without being prepared for almost any eventuality. Now, he needed to change his appearance, and he had the wherewithal in the house to do so; it was a very different-looking El Asesino, with a neat little grey moustache, grey sideboards and grey hair and wearing red-tinted glasses, who left the house shortly after. None of the men now had the appearance of fishermen. All five were neatly dressed in clean shirts and slacks.

Arsenio got in the front of the Panda, with

Carolyn, Hantash and Shannon in the back. Kasar and Springer donned the young couple's crash helmets and climbed on the Harley. They set off first, heading south on a route that had been carefully planned earlier. Five minutes later, Arsenio left in the Panda. The plan was that they would stick to local roads – yellow on the map – for thirty kilometres until they hit the C545, when they would turn south-east towards Santiago de Compostela.

Once they got off the riverside track they would travel – as would the Harley – at a steady ninety kilometres per hour, thus preserving the distance between them. The reason for this procedure was precise and clever: Arsenio was aware that whenever there was a police roadblock in Spain, a kilometre or so before it but on the other side of the road, there would be standing a member of the Guardia Civil, with a machine-gun, waiting to apprehend – and if need be shoot at – any vehicle foolish enough to turn around when it met the tailback leading to the roadblock. Springer had a radiophone with him. So did Arsenio. Should the bike encounter any such obstacle – as Arsenio was convinced it would – Springer would warn Arsenio over the radiophone and he would have plenty of time to turn around and take another route.

In fact, they were lucky. There was only one roadblock, just after the town of Portomouro, and they were able to backtrack and follow fifteen

kilometres of local road to Santiago de Compostela
– where Arsenio was relieved to get stuck in the
comfortable anonymity of traffic jams, and where
he left the silently gloomy Carolyn in the car with
Shannon and Springer to go off and buy her the
pair of trainers and socks she was going to need
for the night's ordeal in front of both of them. He
also purchased for her a long, dark wig, sunglasses,
and green lipstick and eye shadow.

When the stolen Harley-Davidson and the Panda
left Santiago de Compostela to head south-east to
Orense and thence to Verín, near the border with
Portugal, it was after five o'clock, and the heat
of the afternoon was becoming oppressive. They
still had a drive of some two hundred and fifty
kilometres ahead of them.

The Home Secretary's nerves had been at full
stretch ever since the morning's telephone call with
the message from Carolyn. He had got together the
million pounds. It was sitting, in a brown-paper
parcel about the size of four shoe boxes, on the
inlaid, red-leather top of his desk. Since there was
nothing else he could do about his daughter, while
waiting for five o'clock and the next phone call to
come he had been trying to occupy himself with his
most urgent business in hand. His eyes must have
strayed more than a hundred times to that parcel;
one million pounds, money with very considerable
purchasing power, took up a remarkably small

space. He had imagined it would be very much more. It weighed in at about ten kilos and had – the more so perhaps because of the ordinariness of the brown paper and thin string – a strangely hypnotic quality about it.

The afternoon dragged by dreadfully slowly – and then at the appointed hour there was no call from Kirsty. Parker-Reed did not yet know about events down in Spain because Major Fernandez had been too involved with what was going on to take the time to phone him; besides, the major was hoping that when he did call the Home Secretary it would be with good news.

Kirsty had heard from El Asesino. He had called her from the house by the river before departing, with instructions to cancel the arranged message to London until further notice. There was no way until he was clear of the danger area and reorganised that he could begin to collect the ransom money. Let the son of a bitch sweat, had been his words.

Well, the son of a bitch was certainly doing that. Parker-Reed waited until six, rationalizing that England was one hour behind Spain in clock time, perhaps they had not taken that into account. At ten after six, convinced that something had gone wrong, he called the *Mirabelle*.

Fernandez was back aboard, working from Travers Bonnington's office. With him was Pomares. Information, in the form of known histories and photographs of associates of El Asesino, was being faxed through from the London office of Interpol. So far – apart from that of Arsenio himself – Pomares had recognized only one photograph, that of the Irishman, Tim Shannon, who had escaped from Parkhurst with the Venezuelan. 'He was the technician who was going to install the video,' he told Fernandez. 'But he had guns in the box, you understand me?'

The major glanced at Shannon's record. His conviction for rocketing the House of Lords he knew about, since he had been there. The rest was news to him. Suspected – there was no hard evidence but the word more often than not meant guilty – of being involved in eight separate bombings over a period of five years in which, in total, eleven innocent people had died and fifty-three had been injured. Also believed to have murdered by shooting or garrotting several UDA men in and around Belfast. Nice company Carolyn was in, thought Fernandez, grimly.

Parker-Reed rang, and Fernandez brought him right up to date with events. 'Can't you call the Spanish police off?' was the Home Secretary's horrified reaction. 'They're liable to get her killed.'

'It's too late now, sir,' said the major. 'With respect, you called them in yourself. They have a fierce pride – and a good record of success in kidnap cases.' He reminded Parker-Reed of the Melodie case, some seven years before, when the daughter of Armenian-born international businessman

Raymond Nakachian was held for ransom – for a sum of some thirteen million dollars – in the south of Spain, but was finally rescued unhurt after twelve days, with all the criminals being apprehended and no money changing hands.

'Look, I have the first million,' said the Home Secretary, his eyes on the parcel. 'It's on my desk right in front of me. All – listen – all I want to do is pay what they want and get Carolyn back unharmed. Can't you stop the Spaniards from going after them?'

'Excuse me, sir, but I have no power in that direction,' Fernandez reminded him. 'If anybody can do that, it's you.'

'Yes, of course. I'm sorry. Well, I'll try.' He paused. 'Well,' he went on, slowly, 'you've done what you could, Major Fernandez. There's nothing else you can do now that she's on the mainland. You may as well report back to the Chief of General Staff.'

The words – without that being Parker-Reed's intention – knifed into the major. He fought back a rising anger. 'I've just lost a boat and her entire crew apart from the sub men,' he said, keeping his voice steady. 'Your daughter, sir, is one thing – and I'll do everything in my power, given the chance, to see that she comes to no harm. My dead men are quite another. I intend to track down this monster and his gang wherever they might be, and bring them to justice.'

'Yes, well . . .' started Parker-Reed.

'Permission to carry on, sir?' Fernandez broke in.

Something in the hard edge to the SBS man's voice told the Home Secretary that this was no time to argue. 'Permission granted,' he said.

Pomares recognized the face of only one other known associate of El Asesino – Felix Springer. The German had never been convicted of any terrorist activities for the simple reason that he had never been caught, but he was well documented from his days with the Baader–Meinhof gang. Little was known of him since, except for the fact that he had worked with Arsenio for the PFLP. But he had one conviction, from when he was only seventeen. It was for attacking a teenage couple at night in a parked car at a lonely spot in the Black Forest. He had served four and a half years for grievous bodily harm of the young man and rape of the girl. Fernandez did not like that last chilling piece of information one little bit.

It was just before seven o'clock when Pomares boarded the Wessex to be flown back to Malpica. His wife, meanwhile, was lying on a bed, trussed as expertly as the young couple who were being held prisoner with her. Señora Pomares was too frail to fight her bonds for long, but the girl was continuing to struggle helplessly against them every now and again. Pedro had adopted a different tactic. Realizing he had little chance of freeing himself, he had contrived to get on the floor on his back beneath the window and, with his booted feet in the air, was loudly kicking the shutters.

Pedro's Harley-Davidson was at that moment being driven by Felix Springer, with Salim Kasar on the back and, a kilometre or so behind them, the Panda. The little convoy was travelling in a south-easterly direction on the N525. They were approaching the town of Ginzo de Limia, some eighty kilometres from Verín – just beyond which lay the point on the border between Spain and Portugal for which they were all heading.

Had not a man from the rental agency paid a courtesy call on the house by the river, to see that everything was all right for the renters, the prisoners would probably have remained there for days. There was no answer when he tugged the old-fashioned bell-pull, but the crashing of the shutters, which had stopped temporarily, resumed with even greater intensity. He let himself in with a pass key.

Twenty minutes later the Guardia Civil had the number of a stolen Harley-Davidson to look out for, plus the information from Señora Pomares that the kidnappers were also using a white Panda.

The police were one step nearer to detaining the fugitives and Carolyn Parker-Reed. But El Asesino and his accomplices were drawing ever closer to the border.

16

There was only one further brush with a roadblock before they reached Verín. It was just after
Albarellos. Turning back into the town and stopping there to check the map, Arsenio found that
they could in fact go south from there until they
hit the local road he needed to get them close to
the border.

Springer and Kasar were waved through the
roadblock without so much as a glance. Details of
the stolen motor cycle were not to reach the police
there for another twenty minutes, by which time it
would be too late. As they pulled away from the
roadblock, Springer received a call from Arsenio
with instructions to catch up with the Panda at a
little town called Oimbra, some fifteen kilometres
south of Verín. Springer's route was the longer way
around by some six kilometres; for the first time,
the German did what he had been longing to do
– he put the bike through its paces. It went like a
dream.

At eight o'clock on the dot, they met in Oimbra.

They were on a mountain road, surrounded by impressive, pine-clad mountains which reached verdant heights of fifteen hundred metres. There was very little traffic, and it was extremely unlikely they would encounter another roadblock in this wild countryside, but Arsenio was taking as few chances as possible. He told Springer to proceed a kilometre ahead of them once more. They went through the village of Casas del Montes, mountains towering all around them, the narrow road winding and with many precipitous drops – particularly hazardous since the occasional pothole would spring at them on the other side of a blind bend.

As soon as Bousés was a kilometre or so behind them, Arsenio called Springer with instructions to wait for him.

'Get out, Carolyn,' Arsenio told his captive as he pulled the Panda up next to the parked bike. Fear clutched the young woman. They were in a desolate spot, and had seen no other vehicle since leaving Bousés. To their left there loomed a thickly forested mountainside, while the right-hand side of the road dropped away so steeply that the tops of pine trees growing on the upper slope were almost close enough to reach out and touch. For an awful moment she thought that this was the end for her – that they were going to murder her here. They were going to dump her body over the edge, or they were going to bury her. It was astonishing how many dreadful thoughts crammed themselves into her mind within a matter of seconds. She sat, frozen with fear, in her seat.

One of Arsenio's big hands gripped her arm, as the other crossed her waist to open the door. 'Get *out*,' he repeated, this time shoving her.

She stared at him with big, wide eyes. Her lips were trembling. She felt sick. 'But what . . .?'

'It's all right. I'm not going to hurt you,' he interrupted her. He let go her arm and swung his legs out. 'We're going for a bike ride,' he said quite casually. 'Come on.'

'A *bike* ride?'

'That's what I said.' Going around to the rear of the little car, he opened the boot and took out a flight bag. Inside, among a small collection of tools of his trade, were the four Smith & Wesson handguns, Hantash's 9mm CZ75 and a box of ammunition.

Arsenio sounded not in the least menacing – and the fact that he was now carrying a bag somehow reassured her; happily, she was unaware of its contents. There was less fear in her as she stepped out of the Panda – but a great deal of apprehension.

He thrust the heavy bag in her hand. Springer was standing by the motor cycle, holding it up. Kasar had already got into the car. Arsenio took the bars of the bike from the German and climbed on. He put on a helmet – no sense in getting stopped in the last little town before the border by some country bumpkin of a policeman for not wearing it.

'Wear that,' said Arsenio, as Springer handed Carolyn the other helmet. 'Get up behind me. And be very sure not to try any tricks. All that will do is either injure or kill us both.' He jumped on the kick-start. 'See you in São Miguel,' he said to the others. 'Be lucky.'

The engine started with a throaty roar and they were off, travelling slowly, one of Carolyn's arms wrapped tightly around Arsenio's waist, the other hand clutching the bag between them, which, had she only known – and then had she found the necessary courage – contained the means to put a rapid end to her tormentor.

The late evening shadows were lengthening down in the valley far below them to their right. To their left the forested mountainside was beginning to grow dark. The yellowish orange of the darkening sky had a luminous quality to it. The panorama was strikingly beautiful for anyone in the mood to appreciate it; to Carolyn it merely heightened her sense of isolation and despair.

Arsenio was in no hurry; the last village on this road, the outpost of Videferre, was only five kilometres distant and he needed the cover of night for the next part of his plan. It would soon be dark, and it suited him to take his time and not reach the village until it was.

The four in the Panda, on the other hand, were

in a hurry. They had thirty kilometres of winding, mountainous road to negotiate before hitting the C532 once more, and another twenty or so to the border town of Feces de Abajo. They wanted to be across the border – on foot – in time to hire a car in Portugal. They preferred to hire one in a false name to the even riskier alternative of being obliged to steal a vehicle.

Shannon, behind the wheel, had cut his teeth driving – illegally, though scarcely anyone cared in Ireland in those far-off days – on the mountain roads around Killarney. Now he pushed the Panda to its limit. Not that its performance was at all impressive, especially with the weight it was carrying, but even so, on the hazardous road from Bousés to where it joined the C532, it was nothing less than suicidal. Hardened terrorists his passengers might have been, but the Irishman's reckless driving all but scared the life out of them.

Curious faces peered out from the interiors of shabby-looking bars into the dimly lit, cobbled main street of Videferre as Arsenio and Carolyn drove by. Arsenio had taken the precaution, at a battered and barely legible sign telling them they were a kilometre from the village, to stop the Harley and take measures to ensure that Carolyn would not give him any trouble as they passed through. She had protested that she would do no such thing as he tied her wrist to the handle of the flight bag in case she decided to drop it in the street and thus attract attention to them. She further protested as he secured her ankles with string to the footrests. Then he shut her up by gagging her – a fact that would go unnoticed behind the black plexiglass visor of her helmet. He also told her, quite calmly, that if she still managed to draw anyone's attention and they tried to stop the bike, he would shoot them.

They sailed through Videferre without incident, in a couple of minutes. Then the road came to a dead end. There was nothing in front of them but a shaly mountain track, no wider than a footpath, snaking upwards through scrub-covered mountain. Arsenio drove straight up it.

The off-duty policeman who lived in the last house in the village watched the winking, bouncing progress of the bike's lights until they disappeared, high above him. A couple intent on lovemaking, he assumed; it was the perfect night for that sort of nonsense.

After a while, driving on it having become more and more tricky, the track became impassable except on foot. They had reached the side of the mountain. Far below them, just discernible in the dim light from a not quite quarter moon and the brilliant stars, stretched a plain with a river running through it. On the other side of the plain, the distance from them impossible to judge, but certainly several kilometres away, was

the cluster of lights from a village. Arsenio got off
the bike, yanked it on to its stand, untied Carolyn's
feet and took the bag from her.

'Christ,' she said, looking in dismay down into
the void. 'Now what?'

'We walk.'

She softly echoed his words. 'We walk.' She
squinted ahead of them and down. 'But where?
We're on the edge of a bloody mountain.'

'Down there,' he grunted. He jerked his chin.
'Then over there. To Portugal.' He slid the handles
of the bag together up his arm and over one
shoulder, took her hand and started down the
rocky track, tugging her after him.

She resisted, snatching her hand out of his. 'If
you think I'm going down there . . .' she protested.
'We'll break our necks.'

'No we won't. The track carries on. It's an old
cattle and mule track – they're all over these
mountains. It'll wind right the way down into
the valley.' He dug into the bag and brought out
a powerful torch, which he switched on. 'This'll
make it easier.'

'I'm *not* going down there.' Having to some
extent got used to being the prisoner of this man,
she had lost a little of her fear of him – enough,
at any rate, to register her protest firmly.

He sighed as he turned to her and shone the light
directly in her face, blinding her. 'Carolyn, oh but
you are, my love,' he said, insistently but without

menace. 'We both are. You have two choices. You follow close behind me, in which case should you slip you'll have me to fall on. Or . . .' He reached in a back pocket of his slacks and slipped out a flick-knife which he held up between the torch and her face. He pressed a button and a nasty-looking, slightly curved blade sprung open with a menacing click. '. . . you lead the way with this prodding you on. In which case if I slip *I'll* fall on *you. Comprendes?*'

She nodded weakly. He folded the knife and put it away, then again started down, very slowly and carefully, Carolyn on his heels.

The shale was loose, smashed and broken continuously over the centuries by the hard little hooves of hundreds of thousands of goats and lambs, by countless cows, by shepherds' boots and sticks, by donkeys and by horses – and the path was perilously steep. But taken carefully, with the torch picking out their every stepping place, it was safely negotiable. They slowly slipped and slithered their way down, Carolyn tense with the fear of it and even El Asesino not exactly having the easiest of times. Every little bend, each of them fifty or so metres from the previous one and something like twenty below it, was a tight little hairpin so that the nasty drops were continually changing from their left to their right.

Happily, it was too dark to see just how severe those drops were; to ensure they did not, Arsenio was careful to keep his light directly on the path ahead and not let its beam slip over the edge. Very gradually, as their legs began to feel the strain and their feet began to ache and blister, they climbed down towards the plain, where the black, twisting streak of river – the Assureira – bounced silver shards of moonlight and twinkling stars at them as it gradually appeared to broaden and lengthen.

It took them fifty-five minutes to get down, by which time Carolyn felt as weak and shaky on her legs as a newborn foal. Relief to have made it alive surging through her, she sunk down on to the hard, grassy ground, hands between her legs, head drooping, breathing heavily.

'Here.' Arsenio unscrewed its silver-plated top, pulled out its cork and handed her a hip-flask. She looked dubiously at it, then at him.

'What is it?'

He grinned, and she caught the grin in the faint light. It was the first time she had seen him exhibit any trace of humour; shocked at herself for doing so, she noticed that he was unusually attractive with his grin.

'I'm hardly going to poison you at this stage of the game,' he told her. 'Have a sip, you need it. It's twenty-year-old Chivas Regal whisky.'

And he had offered her the flask first, she noted. Somewhere behind this desperate man there lurked a gentleman. She remembered as she drank, spluttered, then drank some more before handing back

the flask, that he had rescued her from rape. Her
fear seemed to have subsided enough to allow her
to look at her captor as a man and not simply as
a dangerous criminal who was trying to trade her
life for money. Suddenly realizing how sore her left
foot was, she took off the trainer and sock. There
was a blister, split and angry, on the ball of her
big toe.

'Shit,' she said.

'Me too.' He dug in his bag and fetched out a
tin of sticking-plasters, opened it and handed her
one, then took off his own right shoe and sock.

'Now what?' she asked, when their feet were
patched up.

'I told you – we're walking to Portugal. It isn't
far.' He took a slug of whisky and offered the flask
to her again. She shook her head.

'Yes – but *then* what?' she persisted.

'Then,' he said, screwing on the top and putting
the flask away in the flight bag, 'if all goes to plan,
we meet my team and we find somewhere to hide
you until your daddy coughs up.'

'Team? Is that what you call them? They're not
exactly sportsmen.' The two stiff swigs of whisky
had gone straight to her head, emboldening her.

He shrugged. 'What do you want me to call
them? My murderous bunch of thugs?'

'Well, they are, aren't they?'

He stared blankly at her. Yes, they are, he
thought. And I'm a thug too, sweetheart. Whether

I like it or not. And I don't very much, but that's what I am. That's life in my jungle. Reaching down, he took her by the upper arm and helped her to her feet.

'We've still got a long way to go,' he told her. 'Let's move. Just shout if you want another snifter.'

Meanwhile, the others, having abandoned the Panda in a side-street in Feces de Abajo, had made it to the border post on foot, and crossed one by one with their false identities without incident. They had caught the only car-hire business still open as it was about to close, and Hantash was at that moment driving them on Portuguese highway 1035, in a southerly direction by the side of the River Támega. There was a mountainous, roundabout route ahead of them to get them to the town of São Miguel, where Arsenio was headed with Carolyn – one hundred and sixty kilometres of it, when in fact São Miguel was just twenty kilometres from where they had parted company outside Bousés.

Three-quarters of an hour later, Arsenio and Carolyn arrived at the Río Assureira. It was wider at that point than he had imagined – and deeper, considering it was July. But then this was mountain country where it rained a lot during the spring, and the streams were still running, feeding the river. He had hoped that they would be able to wade across. He saw that they would, but only some of the way; in the middle they would probably be obliged to swim. He put his bag down on the dried mud bank.

'Strip off,' he told Carolyn, as he began to unbutton his shirt.

'*What?*'

'We're going to have to swim. We wouldn't want to be walking into town with soaking-wet clothes, now would we?'

'No, but . . .' she stared at him. His shirt was off and he was carefully folding it. He had a superbly muscular torso, she could not help noticing.

'No buts, Carolyn. Get your gear off.'

He took off his shoes and socks and stowed them in the bag with his shirt, then unzipped his trousers while she stood, chewing her bottom lip, silently watching him.

'Come *on.*' He finished undressing. 'We haven't got all night, darling. You wouldn't want me to have to help you now, would you?'

Deeply reluctant, but realizing she had no option, she took off her sweater, then the trainers and socks, then the jeans. She did not look at him again until she handed him her clothes. He was naked, making no effort to hide himself from her. She tried to keep her eyes away from his genitals, but they flickered over them twice, seemingly with a will of their own.

He rolled the sweater and trainers and socks in the jeans and tucked the bundle in the side of the bag with his own, carefully folded clothes. Then he held out his hand, looking her in the eye and not at her bare breasts as most men would have done. 'The bikini bottom,' he said.

She flinched. 'That's hardly necessary.'

'Why do you think I've taken my pants off? I don't happen to be an exhibitionist. I don't want wet pants showing through my trousers in the village. I don't want to feel wet. I don't want you with wet pants, either, even supposing nobody in the place is awake when we get there.'

'I'll put them in the bag when we get to the other side,' she said. 'I won't wear them any more.'

He sighed, then produced that infectious grin again. 'Have it your own way,' he told her. 'But you're still going to have to take them off in front of me, aren't you? Tell you what, take them off now, I promise not to look at you, *or* when you put them back on. Take them off on the other side of the river, then I'm going to *ogle* your every move, my lovely. Your choice.'

'Shit,' she said. She was beaten. 'All right – turn your head away.' She hooked her thumbs in the sides of the bikini bottom.

'Just hold it a moment.'

Producing a length of string from the bag, he looped it around her neck.

'What the . . .?' she said, a touch of fear creeping back.

'Hate to do this, but I wouldn't want you getting any funny ideas and trying to swim off.

Behave yourself, stick by my side, and you won't even know you've got it on.' He tied a slip-knot in the string, so that she had a noose hanging loosely around her neck, a couple of metres of string between it and the end of the string in his hand. 'Now you can take your knickers off,' he said, glancing up at the moon.

It was beginning to feel like some kinky sex scene – except that he kept his word and did not look at her. But somehow, as they stepped side by side into the cool, steady tug of the river, she could not avoid sneaking a peep at him, before hurriedly looking away, her mind a confused jumble.

Underfoot were rocks, large pebbles and small stones. All were worn smooth by the water, but picking their way across and through them was tricky because they were slippery and quite invisible; the only view afforded them by looking at the surface of the river was a fractured reflection of moon and stars. The water plucking at their lower legs was cool, just short of cold; in contrast to the sticky warmth of the night, it felt wonderfully refreshing.

For Carolyn, everything was fast becoming unreal again. Nude, stepping out into a dark river dividing Spain and Portugal, hand in hand with a naked killer who had kidnapped her under the sea, a noose around her neck, its end in his hand. Despite it all, her eyes slid sideways and she cast another furtive glance at him. He really did

have a very fine body. As for his co . . . Christ –
what the bloody *hell* was going on in that crazy
brain of hers? She tore her gaze away from him,
determined to look at nothing more than the water
from then on.

Arsenio was acutely aware of her too. It was hard
not to look at her, as the stones and rocks gave way
to fine grains, then a level bed of silt, and the water
rose above their knees and steadily up their thighs.
But he managed the feat. It occurred to him that
when they reached the other bank he could take
her if he was so inclined – and she may even go
along with it without putting up too much of a
struggle. He put the thought firmly from his mind.
He wasn't in the rape business, and only yesterday
he had rescued her from just such a fate. And if
there was one crime he would detest seeing on his
wanted-for list it was that base act.

Then the water was surging coldly above their
waists, the current pulling at them, and they were
swimming, Arsenio's flight bag held above his head
in the hand with the end of the piece of string. By
the time they were almost across and they put their
feet down again on silt, the current had taken them
quite a way downstream. They could just make
out in the dark and deeply shadowed landscape
that they were opposite an olive grove.

There were fewer stones on the river bed than
the other side. But the bank was steeper and they
had a struggle to haul themselves up. They were

in Portugal. The lights of São Miguel, much closer now but still some way away, were tucked into the lower slopes of a mountain, visible above the olive trees.

'You can take the noose off,' said Arsenio, as he dug into the bag and brought out a clean, white T-shirt. He handed it to her. 'Here, dry yourself.' He found a sweater in among the hardware and used it to towel himself down, then he handed her her bundle of clothes and her bikini bottom and started to dress. She actually felt good after the swim. It had cleansed the fishy smell from her body, though the aroma still clung vaguely to the sweater and jeans.

'You like olives?' were his next words as they stepped in among the tightly planted, small, twisted trees. He stopped to pick one.

'I detest them,' she told him.

'It's an acquired taste. Well worth persevering for.' He bit into the olive. 'You should try one.'

'You didn't look at me. Not even once did you look at me.' She sounded surprised, even perhaps the slightest bit regretful.

He grinned flatly at her. 'I never break a promise to a pretty girl.' He paused. 'But you looked at me.'

She felt herself colouring. She hastily changed the subject. 'If you never break a promise, will you promise me you won't hurt me? That I'll get out of this alive?'

He spat out the olive pip and stopped to pick another. 'You'll get out alive. That I promise you,' he told her, popping the olive into his mouth.

'What about not hurting me?'

'Only if you continue to behave yourself. Daddy's going to pay up, I'm sure of that — so there won't be any need for further persuasion in that direction.'

A chill ran through her. 'You would have . . . you *would* have cut my finger off, wouldn't you?'

'I wouldn't, not personally.'

'But that awful, German-sounding thug, he would have done?'

He stared at her regretfully, without expression. 'Yes, he would.'

They walked on in silence until they were almost out of the grove. Through the trees, up ahead, they could make out an upward-sloping field of long grass. Carolyn had more or less lost her personal fear of Arsenio; swimming naked with him, he not looking at her nude body, the sight of his nakedness, his calm and measured way of speaking, all had contrived to make her feel almost comfortable with him. She was his prisoner, yet the fear had almost melted away. Analysing her feelings, she found that she could not even bring herself to hate him. Was this, then, the famous Stockholm syndrome? Surely not — didn't that have to do with a hostage coming round to a terrorist's way of thinking, even beginning to love

185

him, not with a kidnap victim finding things she rather liked about her abductor? She was feeling most odd.

'I don't understand you,' she told him, as they walked from the olive grove to find themselves thigh-high in pale-yellow grass with tiny snails clinging to it. 'A man like you, involved in something like this. I mean, you're hardly an oaf.'

He raised a mild eyebrow. 'An oaf? I hope not.'

'But you've been behaving like one,' she said. Then she added hastily, 'Until we were alone, that is.'

'Carolyn, I'm in charge of a multi-million-pound kidnap operation. I've had the SBS and half the police in Spain after me. Do you expect me to behave like the perfect gentleman?' He realized that he was surprised at himself for opening up to her. He was beginning to like her – and that was not exactly a great idea. She was a spunky young lady – she had been terrified half to death and now she was chatting away with him as if they were old friends.

She gaped at him. 'Multi-million-pound?' she repeated. She knew it had to be a lot of money, but not so much. 'How *many* millions?'

'Five.'

'God, you're going to absolutely skint my poor father.'

'I doubt that. He's a very rich man.'

'And what gives *you* the right to try and relieve

him of his money? He works terribly hard to keep hold of it. Hanging on to your fortune isn't easy these days.'

He frowned at her. 'Look, why don't you just shut it?' he told her, trying to sound menacing, but falling short of it.

Shut it she did, that was until they were through the field. 'I don't even know your name,' she said. 'I don't recall anybody ever calling you anything.'

'It's Arsenio,' he said.

'What sort of a name is that?' She seemed to have heard it somewhere before.

'A Spanish name. I'm Venezuelan by birth.' They were on a stony track, leading upwards, the village now not far away. Gorse and shrubs were closing in on them.

She searched her memory. Venezuelan? Arsenio? Christ! She stopped dead, mouth dropping open. 'You're not *the* Arsenio?' she asked him, knowing at that moment that, of course, he had to be.

'El Asesino,' he said bluntly, not looking at her. '*The* one, yes. The Assassin.'

'*God!*'

'Perhaps now you'll stop being so fucking friendly and quit asking stupid questions?' He was irritated with himself; he did not care for his nickname, neither did he feel like scaring Carolyn again; but he needed to, otherwise he would shortly be softening up – and then slipping up.

She tried to digest the information, but it was

187

not sinking in properly. The world's most wanted terrorist – as Carlos the Jackal had been until he was caught? The man who had blown up the peers' guest room in the House of Lords and two cleaning women along with it? The man who had broken out of Parkhurst and caused the death of the governor in so doing? *This* man – who had been concerned about her feet, and her dignity, and who had saved her from rape?

He seemed to have read her mind, for he said, a minute or so later, 'An enigma, that's me.'

'And how,' retorted Carolyn.

They spoke no more until the track began to widen as they got nearer the village. Suddenly, up ahead, the beams of a car were swinging from side to side, cutting swathes in the blackness, the car itself out of sight but approaching. Taking hold of Carolyn by the elbow, Arsenio hurried her off the track and behind the shelter of some thick gorse, pulling her down so that they were crouching side by side. He unzipped his bag to pull out a Smith & Wesson 459 and a silencer, which he screwed on adroitly.

'Very, very still, and very, very quiet,' he told her. She had no intention of being anything else. The fear was seeping back.

The car, bumping around on its springs, soon came into sight. An oldish Renault 5 with police markings on its side and an unlit blue lamp on its roof, it stopped twenty metres before reaching them. The driver's door opened.

Arsenio was pointing the gun in the policeman's direction. 'Try anything at all to attract his attention, and I shall kill him,' he whispered.

The seeping fear became a flood. Carolyn was as still and as quiet as a sleeping mouse as the policeman had a pee, lit a cigarette and leant back on his car to gaze up at the stars. He smoked some of the cigarette, got back in the car, backed off the track, turned around and headed towards the village.

'Good girl,' said Arsenio, standing and putting the gun away.

She was too scared to say anything. The terrifying fact that she was in the hands of the dangerous killer El Asesino had at last sunk in.

They encountered no one else out in that lonely Portuguese outpost. Apart from occasional flurries of breeze, and the infrequent rustle of night creatures in the scrubby undergrowth that closed in on the track, it was still and quiet. Then, as they neared São Miguel, familiar music, very faint at first, reached their ears. Totally unexpected in so remote a part of Europe, it was the Beatles singing *Penny Lane*.

As the music got louder and they rounded a bend to see, quite close, a cluster of lights, Arsenio again took out his silenced Smith & Wesson and shoved it into his trousers, under his shirt. Then he slipped the handles of the flight bag over his shoulder, took out his flick-knife and opened it. Putting his arm around Carolyn's waist, he slid the knife up under the front of her sweater; her skin crept at the cold touch of wicked steel on her bare belly.

'We're lovers, understand?' he told her. 'A pair of strolling lovers.' He looked at his watch – ten minutes to midnight. There would still be some people around, for sure. Villages this far south tended not to go to sleep early.

The track became a cracked and potholed road. Suddenly they were in a narrow village street, dark-windowed, unattractive little houses on either side of them, here and there a slither of light peeping from behind closed curtains.

It was a tiny, dispirited, one-horse, one-policeman sort of a place – much what Arsenio had expected and hoped for. Within a couple of minutes the road had widened fractionally and they were walking past some tiny shops into the village centre. Ahead of them were the lights of a bar, outside it the car belonging to the one policeman was host to a couple of scruffy-looking, dark-faced men who were sitting on its bonnet, talking and drinking. The music was coming from the bar, the Beatles sounding ludicrously incongruous in this land of the mournful *fado*. There was also, approaching them as *Penny Lane* gave way to *Don't Let Me Down*, walking in an odd, knock-kneed sort of way and with one hand held up and flopping loosely in

190

front of his thin, gaunt face, a boy in his late teens. He came directly up to them. They could see in the light from one of the few street lamps that saliva was dribbling from a corner of his down-turned mouth. Carolyn gasped as he flapped his dangling hand to within inches of her face, staring at her with vacant, yet piercing eyes, and then wandered on by.

'Village idiot,' muttered Arsenio.

Carolyn, tucked into his side, an arm around him and with her hand resting on his shoulder between the straps of the bag, was so full of dread that he could feel her quaking against him. It did not have much to do with the idiot, though he had given her quite a fright; it had to do with the knife blade flattened upwards against her belly, and with the gun tucked in Arsenio's trousers. She knew that if anything went wrong he would use that gun and maybe turn this quiet village street into a blood bath.

The two men perched on the police car had stopped talking and were staring at this couple who had appeared like phantoms in the night as they drew level. One of them called out something. The policeman emerged from the gloomy interior of the bar.

Arsenio stopped walking. He pulled Carolyn into him, pressing himself against her. 'Kiss me,' he said. 'Make it for real.'

Never had lips been more unwelcome, never a kiss more unpleasant. But Carolyn did as she was told and made it appear very much for real; at least he did not thrust his tongue in her mouth.

'Where in the name of the Holy Virgin did they spring from?' asked the policeman of the men using his car as a bench, as he observed this lovers' kiss.

Arsenio broke up the embrace. He smiled at the three men and started walking Carolyn on. 'Lovely night,' he said in English.

'Where are you from?' asked the policeman in Portuguese.

Stopping once more, Arsenio said in English, 'I don't understand.' He shrugged, and grinned. He kissed Carolyn again briefly. 'Good night,' he said to the men, and walked her on.

'These tourists today, they go everywhere,' offered one of the men.

'But, it's odd, isn't it?' commented the policeman. 'I can't remember seeing a foreign car in the village tonight. Where can they be staying?'

The other man drained his glass. 'Who knows? Who cares?' He spat in the dust. 'Foreigners!'

'You're right, Gonçalo. And their car, logically it has to be somewhere.' He gave the retreating backs of Arsenio and Carolyn a last glance, then wandered back into the bar. 'I'll get us another drink.'

There were no more encounters. Another five minutes, and Carolyn and Arsenio were through the village, walking along the dark and narrow road leading into it. Ten minutes after that they rounded a bend, and there, parked on a dried mud verge and pointing towards inland Portugal, was a hired BMW with Hantash at the wheel, and Springer, Shannon and Kasar as passengers.

'Enjoy the walk, did you now, my pretty?' asked the Irishman as Carolyn was pushed in next to him by El Asesino.

17

Something was giving him hell in the region of his kidneys. Major Fernandez knew it had to be a piece of shrapnel, and that was scary. But his wounds went far deeper than a bit of iron in his back; he would not even begin to be on the mend until he had found Carolyn Parker-Reed and taken El Asesino.

It was just after nine a.m. on the morning after the kidnappers had rendezvoused. Fernandez was in his temporary headquarters aboard the *Mirabelle*, occupying Travers Bonnington's office and the time of Gavin, the American's secretary. He was getting somewhere – though perhaps not very far; two fortuitous events had led him to the conclusion that Arsenio and Co., with Carolyn, were no longer in Spain, but had crossed into Portugal.

The first event concerned the Harley-Davidson. The policeman who lived in the tail-end house of the village of Videferre had realized, as midnight approached, that the couple on the motor cycle who had driven up the mountain track earlier that evening had still not returned. He had been about to go to bed, but changed his mind; lovemaking was one thing – but for so long on an uncomfortable mountain? Perhaps something was wrong. It was tricky up there at night, and they may have had some sort of accident. Or perhaps there was trouble with the bike. He got on his own 49cc Honda and started up to investigate.

He found the Harley lying across a gorse bush, flattening it, just before the track veered off precipitously down the mountain. There were two crash helmets lying nearby. When his shouts into the void met with nothing but echoes of his own voice, he climbed on the Honda and hurried back to his house to put in a call to the Guardia Civil HQ in Verín. There was by now no police department in Spain which did not have a note of the number of the stolen motor cycle. The Videferre officer had neglected to take it down – he was more interested in getting permission to organize a search party – and he was sent straight back up the mountainside to get it.

Thus was Pedro Castillo's stolen bike recovered. The second event concerned the Panda. Not being always quite as cautious as Arsenio, his fellow conspirators, when abandoning the car in the border town of Feces de Abajo, had left it blocking the entrance to a garage in a narrow little street. There was an official notice on the garage, proclaiming that cars parking there would be towed away. This, of course had not concerned Shannon when he left it there – parking near the border was difficult and they were in a hurry to get across. He even left the keys in the ignition.

The driver of the police tow truck found it odd that the Panda was unlocked and with the keys in place, and he reported this fact to the officer in charge of his station, who was very well aware that the whole country was on the lookout for a white Panda whose number was unknown. Events went speedily after that. The owner of the closed car-hire business in Carballo was contacted at his house and shown pictures of the three men known to be involved in the Carolyn kidnapping – Arsenio, Tim Shannon and Felix Springer – and had identified Arsenio. The alias El Asesino had used to hire the car was not in Interpol records; at the slightest suspicion that they might be on to a false name of his he buried it and created another. And Arsenio never, ever, used the aliases under which he kept the flats in London and Barcelona for anything but that purpose – not even to buy an air ticket.

It seemed clear that the fugitives had taken themselves and Carolyn over the border the previous evening. But there the trail ended.

Fernandez was getting good cooperation from the Guardia Civil, but in something as close to him as this, he trusted only himself to leave no stone unturned – and, as it was to turn out, he was right to step into the police action. Sipping coffee and pecking with little appetite at buttered toast that morning, he was turning over in his mind the latest information from the police as he studied a detailed map of the areas where the Harley and the Panda had been discovered. He saw something right away that perhaps the police had not put together.

'It's pretty clear what happened here, wouldn't you say, Gavin?' he asked the secretary, his finger following a road on the map.

'Is it, sir?' responded Gavin.

'I would think so, yes. Some of the men walked across the border after abandoning the Panda in Feces de Abajo. Four of them, that would be. The fifth – and I'd wager my commission to the rank of private that that man was Arsenio – took Carolyn as near as he could get to the border after Videferre – here.' His finger stabbed the map. 'They went across the border on foot. They would have to have crossed a river – here. Then, do you see there's a very roundabout route through Portugal to get back to São Paulo? I don't see Arsenio stealing a car in a tiny village – too risky.'

'And there wouldn't be anywhere to hire one,' put in Gavin.

'Exactly. So he was met. The others either hired or stole a car on the Portuguese side of Feces de Abajo, on the border, and drove all the way around . . .' – his index finger, with its clump of black hairs, traced each of the roads – 'to pick him up.' He sighed. 'Then they went off God knows where.'

'Yes, sir. And the Portuguese police?'

'Cooperation is being sought. It will be given, naturally, but it will take a little time. Then they won't know what car to look for.' Fernandez finished his coffee, thinking deeply. Then he said, 'You know, I'm hardly a detective, Gavin. I'm a major in the SBS, a Royal Marine by training. But, by heaven I'll turn twenty-five-quid whore if it leads me to Arsenio.'

Gavin blinked. 'Yes, sir?'

'Get the Wessex on stand-by, would you? Tell the pilot to clear the route for Feces de Abajo.'

Fernandez was in Feces de Abajo and going through customs within two hours. He found the town disagreeable – like its name, which reminded him of shit. The Guardia Civil had already checked with the officers who had been on duty at the customs post the previous evening that two people resembling Springer and Shannon had gone through at about nine, so that part was confirmed for him – not that he had any doubt. So it had been, as he had suspected, Arsenio who had taken Carolyn across.

In the Portuguese side of the town he set about a task which he doubted that the police would get around to until the next day, if at all; he began checking the car-hire places, showing the three faxed photos he had with him. At the fifth establishment he struck lucky; none of the men in the photos had hired a car personally, but someone bearing a close resemblance to Shannon had accompanied the man who had. It had been a mauve BMW hired for a week with unlimited mileage.

Fernandez hurried the information, and details of the hirer, back across the border to the Guardia Civil HQ. Within fifteen minutes of getting through to Interpol he had the confirmation he was seeking. The name on the driving licence, purportedly issued in France, and its number, was false. Who these credentials were being used by was not known, but that did not matter; the mere fact that the licence was false confirmed that that car was the one the police should seek.

Carolyn had been driven south – presumably – through Portugal in a mauve BMW whose number he had – and so would the Portuguese police have very shortly. With any luck, Arsenio and crew would not yet be abandoning the car.

They were back on the trail, but he hoped to God the Portuguese authorities did not go about the affair in a blundering fashion and risk the girl's life.

His back was playing up badly. As he left the police headquarters he saw that there was a small clinic opposite it with X-ray facilities. He almost went in, then changed his mind. What the hell, he thought, I don't want to know. If the shrapnel is closing in on a kidney I don't have time to do anything about it anyway.

18

Tommy Jenkins Esquire was feeling rather pleased with himself. He had pulled off what he liked to think of as a 'nice little number' – and he appeared to have completely got away with it. It was not often when there was a security-van raid that the CID did not quickly find out who was behind it and arrest those responsible – that is, if they were still in the country or in territory with an extradition agreement with Britain.

But he had foiled the bastards this time, he reflected as he lounged in the early-morning sunshine on the deck of his recently acquired twenty-two-metre yacht, the *Miss Molly*, in Estoril harbour, a short way to the west of Lisbon. There had been only three of them involved in the raid, including himself, and it was now seven months since they had carried it out. Two and a half million quid in readies between them and they had not made a single mistake, leaving not a hint of a clue. Of course, Tommy was a number-one suspect, with form in that sort of business as long as your arm. But let them try and prove it. He was on an extended holiday, was your man, with no intention of returning in the conceivable future, a cute little cockney dolly-bird to keep him company, and nobody even had a clue where he was. Not for him the attention-drawing Costa del Sol, packed with villains and crawling with British Bill. Estoril, with its broad expanses of Atlantic-washed beach, its cosy little restaurants and its swish casino, suited him fine and dandy.

'Nice boat,' said a large man on the quayside loudly, admiring the smooth lines of the *Miss Molly*. The remark was clearly directed at Tommy – and Tommy had a well-developed suspicion of strangers. You just never knew.

'Ta,' he muttered, sinking deeper into the puffy cushions of his wicker deck lounger and burying his nose in a day-old *Daily Mirror*.

The man did not go away. 'As a matter of fact I've been searching for just such a boat,' he said.

Tommy glanced up from the newspaper suspiciously. 'Well, she ain't for sale,' he said. The bloke didn't look like Bill. And he had a bit of a funny accent.

'Pity. She would suit me very well.'

'Sorry, mate. I told you, I ain't selling.'

'I may be prepared to offer you a price you couldn't refuse.'

Greedy little ears pricked up. The yacht had been bought cheaply for readies from a skint and desperate Englishman, a big loser in the casino. Tommy was always interested in making a profit – and one boat was much the same as another to him.

'It'd need to be more bread than she's worth,' he said. 'I'm kinda attached to 'er.'

'I'm not short of cash,' the man told him. 'Can I come aboard and take a look around?'

'Sure. Take your shoes off.'

The narrow gangway squeaked and wobbled as El Asesino made his way aboard. As Tommy got to his feet and the two men shook hands, both using false names as they introduced themselves, fifty metres along the quayside, in front of a small ice-cream stall, Springer, Shannon, Hantash and Kasar, huddled around Carolyn Parker-Reed, who had the tip of the German's knife pressed into the back of her sweater, pricking her, watched the proceedings with interest.

They were tired. They had driven the five hundred kilometres south to Estoril through the night, taking it in turns at the wheel, snatching sleep when they could, stopping a couple of times at all-night cafés. Carolyn had hardly slept at all – she seldom could in moving cars – and she felt, and looked, wrecked.

Tommy's dolly-bird was in a bikini below deck, making coffee in the galley. Her name was Sheila, and she was petite and shapely with straight, shoulder-length, brittle, peroxide hair. The point

of her nose was a little too exaggerated and she
had on too much make-up. That notwithstanding,
she oozed a tartish sort of sexuality.

Villain, Arsenio thought, of Tommy as he was
introduced to Sheila. And she's your thirty-years-
younger gangster's moll. He was seldom wrong
about such things. There was no sense in hanging
around and chit-chatting – nor of seeing over the
entire boat. It was, as he had honestly said, exactly
what he was looking for.

'I'll take it,' he said.

'But we 'aven't even . . .'

Tommy was about to say, 'discussed the price',
as, with the silencer of Arsenio's Smith & Wesson
inches from his face, he swallowed his words.

'I said, I'll take it,' Arsenio repeated. 'And I mean
take it, not pay for it.'

'Christ,' muttered Tommy. 'You're a soddin'
pirate – and there was me thinkin' at first you
might be Bill.'

Sheila's shocked giggle was verging on hysterical.
'Shut her up,' Arsenio told him. 'Gag her and tie
her up – with this.' He produced a roll of brown
parcel tape from his pocket.

''Ang on a minute, old son,' Tommy protested.
'You're makin' a cock-up. I'm one of you, ain't I?
Go and nick some honest geezer's boat.'

Arsenio raised an eyebrow. 'One of me? I doubt
that. Now, do as I say. Tie her up.'

'Piss off. Go on, get off my boat.'

Well, he had guts, thought Arsenio. Stepping back a pace, he put a bullet through the unhealthy roll of fat at the side of the man's waist. It shattered the glass front of an oven behind him. As Tommy grabbed his wound, staggering and whining, Sheila screamed. Arsenio cut it off with a slap around her face which sent her reeling.

'Another sound, girl, I'll kill you,' he snarled. 'Do as I told you,' he growled at Jenkins. 'Or the next one won't just scratch you.'

Blood streaming down over his trunks and the side of his thigh, naked fear on his face replacing the defiance, the English crook set about wrapping up his girlfriend in sticky tape. Scared that she might scream again, he started with her mouth, one corner of which was swelling, along with her bruised cheek.

Keeping his gun on the two of them, watching them, Arsenio climbed the companionway until he was head and shoulders out. Waving at the quayside, he cheerily called out, 'Hey, there. Come on aboard. Have a drink.'

Ten minutes later, Carolyn found herself shut in the small master bedroom with the trussed Sheila and the unlovely, leering Springer for company.

El Asesino was in the wheelhouse with Tommy. 'The German with your girlfriend,' he had just told the man, 'happens to be partial to rape. If you don't behave *exactly* as I tell you, I'll let him do what he likes with her. And I'll shoot you again.'

The flow of blood from Tommy's waist had been crudely stanched with cotton wool and a bandage from the ship's first-aid kit, and he was wearing a T-shirt. As he was starting the motors, Hantash and Kasar were casting off while Shannon, who had done most of the driving, relaxed in the Englishman's wicker lounger. Kasar had taken off his shirt and Shannon had stripped to plain blue underpants. As the *Miss Molly* began to slowly slip through the waters of Estoril harbour, she looked like any other pleasure boat going out for the day with a handful of holidaymakers aboard.

'All you needed to do, like, was be friendly, wasn't it?' Tommy was complaining as he steered the boat out into the Atlantic. He had recognized Carolyn — he could hardly have failed to, since her photograph took up half the front page of his yesterday's *Daily Mirror*. 'Like I said, I'm one of you. All you 'ad to do was cut me in, not bleedin' shoot me.'

Arsenio grinned flatly. 'Tough titty,' he said.

Down below, Carolyn had drifted into a fitful sleep. Her sweater had rucked up over her bare belly, and Springer cast a lustful eye at her smooth, brown flesh. Just give me half a chance, he was thinking. Just half a chance.

19

She was called the *Agincourt* and her presence
in Malpica harbour had drawn quite a crowd.
She was a Royal Marine Offshore Patrol Boat
manned by a crew of SBS commandos with some
Royal Navy matelots to do the rough work, and
she was at Malpica to pick up the submersibles
Shark and *Squid*. The sheer size of her and her
clean, modern lines made the fishing boats in
the harbour – which included the damaged *La
Señorita Juanita*, about to be lifted out of the
water for essential repairs to her hull – look like
clumsy little toys. Unlike the lost *Gremlin*, she
was an obvious military machine, bristling with
guns. There were two housings on each side of the
stern of the boat, where her own submersibles were
normally carried. Today, the housings were empty,
her customary two little submarines left behind at
Portsmouth.

The Wessex helicopter which Major Fernandez
had been using was parked on deck, while the
major himself was in the control room of the ship,

watching as lift lines were attached to the *Shark*, piloted by Corporal Bright. They had been lucky; beaching the submersibles could have damaged the props, but they had sunk into soft mud and were functioning perfectly well.

As the *Shark* was being winched up, water streaming from her, a sergeant brought Fernandez the fax he had been waiting and hoping for. Having attended a funeral service at sea for the lost commandos of the *Gremlin*, aboard the *Agincourt*, with Travers Bonnington and his crew joining in from the deck of the *Mirabelle* alongside, the major was in the dourest of moods; the fax, from the Guardia Civil HQ in La Coruña, served to shake off a little of that gloom. The Portuguese police had found the hired BMW, parked near the entrance to Estoril harbour. It was locked, and they had not tried to open it; instead there were undercover agents keeping a close watch on it, waiting to pounce on anyone who approached the vehicle.

Fernandez digested the welcome information, and then gave it considerable thought. Just how efficient were Portuguese plain-clothes policemen? They were dealing with highly experienced terrorists. With men possessed of the keenest of eyes as far as detecting members of the forces of law and order was concerned. It was most probable they would never approach the car again. He thought some more. Estoril harbour. Boats. El Asesino had something of a penchant for boats – the houseboat used in the attack on the House of Lords; the fishing boat from this very harbour. Both of them hijacked with their owners aboard. It seemed highly likely he may have pulled a similar stunt for the third time. But were the Portuguese police going to investigate thoroughly enough to discover if this was the case? Somehow, he doubted it.

He winced with pain and grabbed at his back. Christ – was he killing himself? Well, he'd die in the attempt to avenge the crew of the *Gremlin*. The pain subsided. He made up his mind on the next course of action.

'Tell the Wessex pilot to prepare for take-off,' he told the sergeant. 'We're going to Portugal – as far south as Lisbon – so he should plan a refuelling stop.'

Outside on the starboard stern, the *Shark* was being made fast, and Bright was crawling out of the hatch. The *Squid* was already having lines attached in preparation for her lift out of the water.

Fernandez realized it was a fair distance to Estoril. He checked it on the map: almost three hundred nautical miles. Flat out, the *Agincourt* could be in the Lisbon area in about twelve hours. Officially, he should take orders from above to move her south, but there was no time to lose.

'Tell Captain Wingfield to make tracks out of here for Estoril as soon as the other submersible's aboard,' he said to the sergeant as he made to leave the control room for the Wessex. Its rotor was already starting to turn. 'Fast as she can go.'

It was ten minutes past two.

In London, the Home Secretary was in the depths of despair. Still no word from the kidnappers. And the goddam million-quid parcel was sitting there on his desk in front of him, taunting him, mocking him. It was now twenty-one and a half hours since he was supposed to have received telephoned instructions about what to do with the money. He had slept very little. He had not shaved. He had neglected his work. Time had passed with the speed of a bicycle being pedalled through desert sand.

All Stephen Parker-Reed knew about his daughter was that she had been hustled off a fishing boat in some backwater called Malpica, and there the trail had been lost. It was all very well for Major bloody Fernandez to say that Carolyn had been smuggled over the border into Portugal. But where was the proof of that? Nobody at all had reported actually seeing her.

He could not get the thought out of his mind that she was dead. They had killed her and abandoned their project. It was illogical, but the dreadful idea would not budge – it was weighing him down. His haunted eyes, dark circles emphasizing the bags beneath them, kept darting from his private telephone to the brown-paper parcel, and back again. He felt he was about to go insane.

Carolyn was, at that very moment, reading a message from a sheet of paper that Arsenio had given her, into his radio telephone. In Barcelona, Kirsty was recording it. It was short and simple, and this time El Asesino had not found it necessary for his purpose to make his prisoner appear to be terrified. Like her father, she had hardly slept in two days. She sounded quiet, subdued and utterly miserable.

'Dear Papa,' she read, 'I have been moved. I don't know where to. They are not feeding me, and they are giving me only water to drink. Do exactly what they tell you, Papa, because they are not going to feed me until all the money is paid.'

Carolyn was staring through a porthole as she dictated this. They were moored perhaps a hundred metres from a sandy beach, in a small bay. There were a few other boats around. People were swimming or water-skiing; others were taking the sun on the beach.

It seemed to be an uncrowded little holiday paradise.

20

By five-fifteen, Major Fernandez, his back giving him frequent, nasty twinges but not seemingly worsening, was walking into Estoril harbour. It was a superb afternoon, the sun not hot enough to be uncomfortable, a gentle breeze blowing the pennants on the boats, a tinkling and creaking in the fresh, clean-smelling air.

The major opted not to announce his presence to the Portuguese police, deciding that such a move would probably only complicate his mission. He was not particularly interested in seeing the BMW either – that was hardly going to achieve anything. He set about strolling around the harbour, asking pertinent questions to everyone he came across who was not obviously a tourist. He could stumble by in Portuguese – it was very similar to Spanish – besides which many of the yachts in the harbour were British-owned. His size, his commanding yet polite manner, stood him in good stead. He was looking, he claimed, for his daughter, who he believed was staying on a boat there, but he did not know which one. His description of the girl was that of Carolyn Parker-Reed. Had anyone seen her; or had any boats gone out today that she might have been on?

It was little more than an hour before he stumbled on what seemed to be what he was seeking. A Spanish couple with a small yacht near where the *Miss Molly* had been moored had noticed some men, with a girl who matched Carolyn's description, go aboard early that morning. Shortly afterwards, the *Miss Molly* had left harbour. The couple had not paid much attention to this, for boats were always moving in and out, but they did think that the girl had not been on deck when the Englishman's yacht left.

Fernandez was a most thorough man. Despite feeling miscast in his role of detective, he continued for another hour with his questions until he had done a complete tour of the harbour, just in case there was any other possibility. There seemed to be none. The *Miss Molly* had not returned by the time he was finished, neither had her master checked her out through customs as intending to take a route leaving Portuguese waters, so she was probably not very far away. The major could have her searched for by local police patrol boats, but he did not feel that was the way to go about it. A stealthy search was the answer, and he could initiate that by hiring a private boat. But it would be dark in a couple of hours so there was not much sense in it.

Better to await the arrival of the *Agincourt*, sometime during the night, and set off at first light.

When, by nightfall, the *Miss Molly* had failed to return to harbour, Fernandez was convinced he was right: that Carolyn was being held prisoner aboard her. A call to the Home Secretary in London added to that conviction. Parker-Reed, he learned, had had a message that Carolyn was safe and he had left his office, destination – as far as his secretary was concerned – unknown. He had taken the brown-paper parcel with him.

Meanwhile, no matter that the entire police force of both Portugal and Spain were now on alert for him, Arsenio had travelled the way he always did. Using one of his perfectly developed aliases, he boarded a plane in Lisbon and flew to Barcelona, arriving at seven o'clock that evening. Kirsty was there to meet him, and at first she failed to recognize him because of his neat little greydyed moustache and the absence of beard. Also, he appeared drawn, older.

'He's going to follow instructions?' he asked her in the taxi.

'Oh, for sure,' she said. 'You can't believe the relief in the poor sod's voice when he knew his daughter was still alive.' She was getting bored with hanging around, pleased to see her lover.

'Good.' That's the way he wanted it. Still, there was absolutely no guarantee that Parker-Reed was not going to try something tricky; he had, after all, direct access to some of the finest police in the world – and a daughter was one thing, but five million pounds, however much you adored her, quite another.

In the flat in Las Ramblas, Kirsty prepared Arsenio his first civilized meal in nearly three days. With lovemaking at the forefront of her mind, she coaxed him early to bed – not a difficult task. But he was exhausted. She tried the one act which never failed to arouse him, but it had the opposite effect. El Asesino dropped into a deep sleep while being fellated – for the first time in his life.

21

La Sagrada Familia, dominating the otherwise unprepossessing, rather dreary square named after its designer, Antonio Gaudí, has variously been seen as a magnificent folly, a misplaced piece of Disneyland, or a masterpiece of Art Nouveau architecture. Constructed almost seventy years ago, the church's main shell was unfinished at the time of Gaudí's death, in 1926, and has remained the subject of municipal alterations, of public rows, and a centre of touristic interest ever since. It was still unfinished, parts of its interior still being worked on, when it attracted Arsenio's attention.

El Asesino had decided that La Sagrada Familia ideally suited his purpose for the first drop, for three reasons. First, there was a small park in front of its entrance from which all movements in, out and around it could be easily observed. Second, there were some areas under construction inside where a flight bag might be concealed for a brief period. Lastly, there was a way out – not a public one but usable – at the back, where there ought to have been a small garden but where there was a clutter of builders' materials instead.

He had finally made it with Kirsty, but not until they woke up the next morning, and now, as he approached the Plaza Gaudí, he was feeling refreshed, totally alert and ready for any eventuality.

The Home Secretary, he calculated, would be on his way from a different direction, in a taxi, at that very moment. Arsenio had covered the twenty-odd blocks north-west from Las Ramblas on foot. Parker-Reed's first instruction, from Kirsty the previous day, was that on arrival at Barcelona airport early that morning, he should take a cab into the city centre, where he was to pick up an envelope waiting in his name for him behind the Bar Central, in the Gran Via. That envelope had contained a plan of the interior of La Sagrada Familia and instructions to deposit his parcel in a corner where some works were being carried out. The parcel was to be in a plain brown flight bag, he was to make sure he was not being observed by any tourist or official before dropping the bag behind a particular tarpaulin – and then he was to leave the church immediately. Should he not leave, the pick-up would not be made and his daughter's agony would be prolonged.

Arsenio, as he lingered at a kiosk in front of the park on the other side of the road from the entrance to the church, taking his time about buying postcards, presented a curious sight. Wearing flower-patterned cotton shorts, sandals with blue socks, a flashy shirt, a panama hat, a camera with powerful telescopic lens around his neck and a luminous yellow rucksack on his back, he resembled a particularly tasteless example of the American tourist. His strategy was a simple one; a man drawing so much attention to himself would hardly be the one waiting to pick up a million-pound ransom. The unusual precaution was in case Parker-Reed had clandestine company.

And the Home Secretary did have company – in spades.

A drab, sea-green tour bus which had to be at least thirty years old, battered and listing slightly to one side, rounded a corner; incredibly, it bore Polish number-plates. It pulled to a wheezy stop, blocking off Arsenio's view of the huge, square, glass-panelled doors of the church. The canti-levered, grey stone-columned portico loomed up forty metres above the roof of the bus, framing, high over the doors, immense, modernistic statues of saints, one on his knees with a cross on his back (or was that supposed to be Christ?). Christ on the cross, thin and dramatic, was on a ledge above them. Higher still, soaring to the heavens, but with a huge crane in the background between them, were four slim and elegant, oddly decorated turrets with holes and bumps in them, and orange and green triangular designs towards their tips which looked like lollipops with balls stuck all around them and crosses on their faces.

The bus disgorged its passengers – as dowdy in appearance as Arsenio was flashy – and creaked off on its way to find an official parking place. Paying for his postcards, Arsenio stiffened. Two things had happened at the same time. A taxi had pulled up and the man who was getting out of it and paying, tall and stooping, was Stephen Parker-Reed; he was carrying a brown flight bag. Another man, who had been sitting on a bench near the kiosk, reading, folded his newspaper and stood. His head was moving around as if he were idly glancing about him while deciding what to do next, but there was something about the slight jerkiness of that movement which suggested that his eyes were holding still on something – and that that something was a somebody: the Home Secretary as he walked up the steps to the doors of La Sagrada Familia. Arsenio went on red alert. Policeman. He glanced around. Not the only one, either: the gardener pruning a tree behind him in the park – something seemed to be not quite right about him; and there was another man pushing a refuse cart who just did not have the look of a street cleaner.

Arsenio's eyes swept the balconies to the left and right of the park. There was a man standing on one of them, leaning over its edge. Well, he might simply be a man on a balcony, watching the world go by below him. Or he might be a man on a balcony with a gun.

Parker-Reed vanished through the doors of the church. Arsenio's eyes were everywhere but on him. He lit a Camel. He had, in fact, managed not to smoke for more than twenty-four hours; now he lit the cigarette, hardly aware of what he was doing.

The Home Secretary, totally uncharacteristically for a man who was perfectly at home with heads of state and royalty, felt nervous as a kitten crossing a busy road. He was unhappy about this stake-out. He just wanted to leave the money where instructed and follow instructions for the next drop as soon as possible. But he had his obligation to Interpol, who were backing him up in any way possible. And, as head of the Home Office – the government department responsible for law and order – he was obliged to cooperate in every way possible to bring the murderer of a ship's complement of SBS commandos to justice.

He had been assured that nothing at all would be done to jeopardize Carolyn's life, and that if the man going to pick up the money turned out to be Arsenio, they would merely follow him to try to discover her whereabouts. Only if it was someone else would they move in to make an arrest and put the sort of pressure on the kidnapper to break him. Nevertheless,

Parker-Reed was in mortal fear for his daughter's safety.

From the kiosk, El Asesino watched as the man who had been on the bench – thickset and wearing jeans, trainers and a yellow T-shirt bearing the legend 'Real Madrid' – walked briskly up the steps and into the church. Over the T-shirt the man had on a loose-fitting, black cotton waistcoat. Arsenio caught a glimpse of a brown strap through the back of the waistcoat's armhole as it jumped on his big shoulders. That confirmed his suspicions. The character was tooled up; he was a cop, for sure.

Walking up the steps at a leisurely pace, Arsenio stopped twice to pretend to take photographs. On the top step, he swung round, flicked the barely smoked Camel away, and pretended to take more shots from there. The gardener, he observed, was actually only making the motions of clipping twigs off the orange tree, while the street sweeper was leaning on his hand cart, smoking, watching the front of the church. The man on the balcony was still there and from his raised position – the steps went up four metres – Arsenio saw the shape of what could very well be a rifle lying at his feet. He smiled tightly to himself as he entered the lofty, slight gloom of the interior of La Sagrada Familia. No way these clowns were going to outwit him.

The church was bustling with tourists, but not so packed that Arsenio could not see across the vast entrance area to the place where the Home

Secretary was to leave the bag. Parker-Reed was most unlikely to make a mistake about the spot, for there was a stone statue of a saint to its left, and it was roped off with red-and-white-striped plastic tape.

Arsenio had been very careful about the exact location of the drop, having posed briefly at the start of the working day, and before leaving his message at the Bar Central, as a municipal inspector following progress of the works. Nothing further was scheduled to take place there for several days – it was perfect for his purpose.

Parker-Reed had already left the money there, having put the bag at his feet and carefully heeled it backwards to behind a red tarpaulin hiding the work area. As Arsenio moved across the stone floor, still pretending to take pictures, following instructions the Home Secretary hurried towards him, on his way out. He passed the kidnapper without a second glance, his face an exhausted mask of worry.

And there was the man in the Real Madrid T-shirt, to one side of the stone saint, face upturned to its haloed head, but eyes darting everywhere.

Adiós, my friend, thought El Asesino.

Guns are basically very simple mechanisms consisting of a mechanically operated firing device, a chamber for a bullet, a clip for more ammunition, and a hollow steel tube through which the bullet is expelled. Arsenio's 35mm SLR camera, with its

70–210mm zoom lens, was just such a contrivance. Skilfully converted for him by a superb gunsmith in a Cairo backstreet three years previously for use as an instrument of assassination, it had nevertheless only ever been used for practice purposes. The film compartment housed its clip of six .20-calibre bullets – small but perfectly lethal, capable of penetrating body armour. The lever which moved the film on, slotted bullets one at a time in front of the firing pin. The pin was operated by the little chrome button normally used for shooting pictures, not people. The zoom lens housed the barrel and worked as a silencer. It actually had a darkened glass lens in it, with a small, round hole, almost invisible, behind which was the business end of the barrel.

Arsenio's camera was as neat a piece of hardware as had ever been invented; it even housed a telescopic sight, through which he had watched the 'gardener'. It had cost him an arm and a leg, but he knew that one day it would prove to be invaluable – and this was going to be that day. He aimed it at the statue, then panned it slightly sideways until the tiny cross-hairs of the telescopic sight were centred on the plain-clothes man's forehead.

El Asesino waited until there was a surge of people around the man, then he slowly depressed the button. There was a faint plop and a slight recoil.

The policeman was actually looking directly at him as Arsenio lived up to his nickname. He was starting to have vague doubts about the flashily dressed tourist; anyone was suspect, even such a tasteless creature, he was thinking. It was the last thought he would ever have. The .20 bullet drilled a neat little hole in his forehead, emerging from the back of his head deflected so that it finished its trajectory by hitting the statue.

Arsenio was moving before the man crumpled to the floor. A woman screamed. All nearby eyes were on the fallen man, who was on his back, his waistcoat open to reveal the shoulder-holstered pistol, blood surging from the holes in his head and spreading over the stone floor. Nobody noticed the garish tourist remove a brown flight bag from behind the tarpaulin and hurry off with it towards the rear of the church.

As soon as Arsenio reached a quiet area, just before the door which he knew could be tricked open to let him out, he hurriedly transferred the bulky parcel of money from the bag to his yellow backpack. When he was through the door, he dropped the bag behind a pile of bricks and made his way unhurriedly among the heaps of building materials, past the foot of the crane, and into the dusty street.

El Asesino had his first million quid. He was only slightly unhappy that he had needed to kill to get it, for he had a deep, almost instinctive, detestation of policemen.

After lunch at a sunshaded table in Las Ramblas,

he was busying himself putting the final touches to the guitar he had brought out of Parkhurst Prison with him when Kirsty phoned London to see if the Home Secretary had returned and was ready to receive his next instructions.

22

It had occurred to Major Fernandez to take the *Agincourt* south in his search for the *Miss Molly*. He could, of course, have used the Wessex as well, but he decided against this; a helicopter buzzing yachts might well have put the kidnappers on their guard. This time, if he located them, he intended to proceed with the greatest of stealth.

He ordered his Offshore Patrol Boat to operate far enough from the beaches so as not to be immediately recognizable for what she was, but close enough in to be able to pick out the names of pleasure craft near the shore with her high-powered telescope.

Heading south, he realized after two hours, had probably been a mistake. He had rounded the Cabo Espichel and taken the *Agincourt* past many little bays with their backdrop of pine-forested mountaïns. South of there was a nature reserve and several kilometres of unprotected beaches. Any boat moored there for long on its own – as it would be – would draw far more attention than if it had company. These people would not make such a mistake. Fernandez ordered the boat to turn around.

It was lunch-time when they passed the point they had started out from, going west. Soon after that they were rounding the Cabo Raso and sailing north. Once again, pine forests were cloaking the inland hills, to the east, on the Serra Sintra.

Fernandez's patience was rewarded late in the afternoon, at almost the same time as Stephen Parker-Reed, back in his London office, was listening carefully to Kirsty's telephoned instructions on how he was to dispose of the second million-pound parcel which was already on its way to him by special messenger from Lloyds Bank. The *Agincourt* had just passed the popular beach of Praia de Samarra, after which there was a smallish cove.

And there she was, moored a couple of hundred metres or so out. The *Miss Molly*.

Under Fernandez's orders, the captain of the patrol boat took his craft straight by. When they had left the cove behind them he started heading in towards the shore.

Among the many useful extras carried by the *Agincourt* were two miniature one-man motor cycles with tiny wheels. The major had them loaded on to the dinghy tender. Corporal Bright and Sergeant Shale were assigned the duty of checking out the *Miss Molly*. In T-shirts and shorts, they took the dinghy in, beached it, and carried a mini-bike each up to where there was a small track running parallel to the sea, where they mounted the bikes and set off on the short trip to Praia de Samarra. There, they hired a pedalo.

As, shirts removed, side by side they pedalled the boat slowly out towards the *Miss Molly* in a sea which had an agreeable swell to it, with a warm breeze brushing them and sunshine streaming over them, either one of the men, in different circumstances, might have remarked on their 'cushy number'. But they were both still deeply affected by the violent deaths of their fellow commandos and they made their way in virtual silence.

They were not alone on the water. There were two speedboats, one pulling a water-skier, several other pedalos, there was a jet-ski roaring around, an angler's skiff and another moored yacht. Their cover as a pair of holidaymakers was every bit as good as that of Arsenio's hijacked yacht.

Felix Springer and Tommy Jenkins were the only people on the *Miss Molly*'s deck. The Englishman had behaved admirably, giving no trouble whatsoever and cooperating as if he were a part of the gang instead of their prisoner – which he fervently wished he were. As the pedalo neared them, Sheila came up from below, wearing a white bikini. Once Tommy had convinced them the day before that his dolly-bird would behave herself, she had been released. In any case, Arsenio had reasoned that

228

almost any innocent pleasure craft had at least one female aboard, and their cover would be so much the better if Sheila appeared a lot on the deck and went about the normal things, like swimming and sunbathing, that holidaymakers did. This decision had had one unforeseen consequence; her tight little, near-nude body had been exciting Springer all day. And he had more or less decided that, during the coming night, he was going to relieve his needs – not with Sheila, however, but with the delectable Carolyn Parker-Reed.

People on pedalos have a habit of inquisitively approaching moored yachts. Several had already passed very close to the *Miss Molly*, the kidnappers ignoring them. They took no notice of Corporal Bright and Sergeant Shale, either.

'Jesus Christ,' muttered Bright as they drew within spitting distance of the yacht at the same moment as Shannon came up on deck. 'It's the bloody Irishman.'

Both commandos had committed to memory the photos of the men known to be working with Arsenio. There was no doubt that the one who had just appeared was Shannon, even though he had dyed his hair and changed its style.

'And *that's* the German,' said Sergeant Shale, hardly able to believe that their task was proving this easy. 'Bugger me.'

They circled the yacht once only, hoping to get a glimpse of the Home Secretary's daughter through a porthole, but drew a blank. But it was not of great consequence; she was surely on board somewhere. And here, lounging around in the sunshine, were the bastards who had murdered their fellow commandos. Well, let them lotus-eat while they could – their nemesis was very close.

They turned the pedalo in a wide arc and headed back towards the beach. There were white flecks far out in the Atlantic, suggesting that the sea was about to get rough.

They waited impatiently until almost midnight. The sky had clouded over and the breeze had filled out into a light wind, but the sea had not turned as stormy as it threatened earlier; it was just a bit choppy.

Fernandez had worked out his strategy most carefully. Strictly speaking, the submersibles were two-men craft, but a third could be squeezed in and the three would not be too uncomfortable over a short distance. Bright was to navigate the *Shark*, Shale the *Squid*. The two commandos who squeezed in with each of them just before the craft were lowered from their frames over the stern were wearing black wetsuits, black rubber plimsolls and gloves, their faces were blacked with grease, and they were armed with Browning 9mm side-arms in waterproof holsters and with stun grenades – and protective goggles and earplugs against the possible effect of those grenades upon themselves.

Fernandez had decided against anything more potent, such as Sterling sub-machine-guns; Carolyn Parker-Reed was on board, as were another innocent couple, and machine-guns sprayed ammunition all over the place. He remembered with regret the death of the woman trussed in the houseboat when he had arrested the House of Lords bombers. He had complete faith in the four operatives who were going in. They were highly trained in all forms of combat, even jungle warfare. Against four unsuspecting kidnappers – with luck, asleep – the pistols and stun grenades should be more than effective.

The submersibles settled down into the water, Bright and Shale started the engines and a diver climbed on to each to disconnect the tow lines. A minute later, with Fernandez clutching his lumbar region and wincing with pain while watching the submarines and praying for both the success of the operation and for himself, the *Shark* and the *Squid* disappeared beneath the Atlantic.

'Make not one sound,' warned Springer, on board the *Miss Molly*. He had unlocked and opened the door of the cabin in which Carolyn was imprisoned so quietly that she had not awakened. Now her eyes flickered open into the blinding glare of a torch. Accompanying the terrifying words was the glint of steel as a knife blade was thrust within inches of her nose. She whimpered, but she did not shout.

'This time, my pretty,' breathed the German.

'This time I have you. But you will enjoy it, you will see.' He laid the large torch down on a shelf so that its light washed over Carolyn's bunk. Keeping hold of the knife, he unzipped his jeans and stepped out of them, watching her with lustfully glinting eyes. She had pulled her sheet up to her chin, and it was trembling on her. Beneath it she was nude. Suddenly, she was dreadfully aware of that nakedness.

'Arsenio will kill you. He . . . he'll shoot you,' she managed.

'Hah. Arsenio, he is far away, *mein Schatz*.' Springer climbed out of his underpants. At least he was not ready, she saw. Maybe he would not manage it. Fat chance, she thought, grimly. She was scared, she was appalled – but she was not, as she had been on that other occasion, scared witless. To a certain extent she had become accustomed to these awful people – and she had been half expecting something like this. Well, no way she was going to take the oft-given advice to lie back and enjoy it. She was not going to give in to this brute without one hell of a struggle. She steeled herself for a fight.

Carolyn totally surprised the German by passively peeling the sheet off her body and dropping it on the floor. He had been sure he was going to have to rip it off her – indeed would have enjoyed doing so. 'You win,' she sighed, rolling on to her back. 'Come on then – you haven't even got it up yet. I'll help you.'

He put the knife by the side of the torch and knelt on the bed between her feet. Taking a deep breath, she brought the ball of her foot up with all her force into his genitals. He howled once, doubling over and clutching at himself. As his eyes raised to her, his face contorted with pain, there was the light of madness mixed with lust in them. 'For that, there is nothing I do not do to you,' he gasped.

'We're almost beneath her,' said Corporal Bright to Sergeant Shale over the sub-to-sub Marconi Modular System. The *Miss Molly* was a blip slap in the middle of his radar screen. 'My men are going on duty now.'

'Roger. Mine too,' said Shale.

One by one the commandos, not wearing breathing gear or flippers, for the yacht was only a couple of metres above the submersibles, went through the cramped, bullet-shaped airlocks below the conning towers and pushed themselves off the decks to glide to the underside of the *Miss Molly*, two on each side, just their heads bobbing above the choppy surface of the sea.

One man in each pair had with him a thin line with a heavily foam-padded, rubber-covered grappling-iron on the end. The ship's rail was low enough to the water for the grappling-irons to need only a light toss to hook on to it. They landed with barely audible thuds. Quiet as shadows, their shoulder holsters unclipped, the commandos shinned up the ropes and crept on to the deck.

Hantash and Springer were the only two of the kidnappers awake. Hantash was in the small stateroom, watching a movie on satellite television. He thought he heard an unusual creak somewhere above him, but he took little notice. Springer was too preoccupied to pay attention to anything but what he was bent on doing to Carolyn Parker-Reed. The pain in his testicles subsiding, he had leapt on her, flattening her on the bunk. She had turned into a furious tigress, scratching and biting and kicking. But she was fighting a losing battle, for he was far too strong for her. What was more, her naked body, and the sexual struggle, had done the trick for him – he was ready to take her.

The door which gave access from the bridge to below decks had a slight creak to it. Highly trained terrorist Hantash heard that creak as one of the SBS commandos eased it open, and he was on his feet with his Czechoslovak 9mm CZ75 at the ready in two seconds. He woke up Salim Kasar, who had fallen asleep watching the film. The Syrian, instantly on full alert, reached for his Smith & Wesson.

A commando was standing, out of sight, on either side of the door as it swung slowly open without another creak. One of them had pulled the pins out of two stun grenades. Only his arm appeared above Hantash as the Palestinian started up the stairs. Recognizing the lobbed missiles for what they were, Hantash took the stairs at a rush, firing his gun. As, going through the door, he was hit by three 9mm bullets almost simultaneously and started to fall, the final shot from his CZ75 smashed the thigh-bone of one of the commandos.

The cardboard stun grenades went off one after the other with great flashes of bright light and deafening noise. Kasar dropped unconscious to the stateroom carpet. Shannon, who had been asleep in an adjoining cabin with the door open, and was woken by the din, had leapt from his bunk, grabbed his gun and then heeled over as the blast of noise and light hit him.

The effect of the grenades lasted for only six to seven seconds – but plenty of time for Shannon and Kasar to be put in handcuffs. However, the blast was only efficient in an open area. Carolyn's cabin was at the end of a short companionway – and the door was closed. When, seconds later, a commando burst through it, brandishing his Browning, Springer was standing with naked Carolyn held tightly against the front of his body, his beefy arm hooked around her neck.

'Drop the shooter,' he grated. 'Or I break the girl's neck.'

Carolyn did something that she could never in her wildest dreams have imagined doing – or even imagine she could possibly have the courage for.

But just moments before she had been crushed beneath the German, furiously fighting him as he was almost reaching his goal of raping her. That fury continued to seethe and rage within her – and her right hand, she saw, was within reach of Springer's knife. She seized it and plunged it behind her with all her force, deep into his side, slicing through a kidney.

He screamed, let her go and sank to his knees, clutching his potentially fatal wound, moaning in agony, blood streaming through his fingers.

Carolyn had never heard a man scream before. There was something unearthly about it. She stared in horrified fascination for long moments at the bloodstained knife in her hand, then at the man who was keeling over at her feet. Her eyeballs rolled upwards so that only the whites of her eyes were showing, the knife dropped from her hand and she fainted away into the arms of the rescuing SBS commando.

23

The horns of Fernandez's dilemma were spread wide and needle-sharp. One of the kidnappers – Joseph Hantash – was dead. Another, the German, was dying from a stab wound. Two more were in custody. Fernandez had rescued the Home Secretary's daughter – but the man he wanted more than he had ever wanted anything in his life, El Asesino, remained free. It had been the Venezuelan who had thrown the grenades which had done for the *Gremlin* and all aboard her, bar himself – and a nasty bit of one of those grenades was threatening to put an end to the major even now.

His immediate duty was to let Stephen Parker-Reed know that Carolyn was safe and well. He was aware that the Home Secretary was due to arrive in Lisbon early the following morning, where he had been ordered to make the second drop. That transaction would be Fernandez's chance to capture Arsenio. But once Parker-Reed knew that his daughter was free, there would be no need for that ransom payment. Therefore, could the major feasibly delay relaying the news until after the drop was made? That was the spread of the horns. Should he take such an unlawful action, he would be subsequently carpeted for sure – Arsenio in custody or no. He would be demoted, possibly reduced to the ranks, or even dismissed from the service. That was the sharpness of the horns.

He agonized for a long time over his gamble: the chance to seize El Asesino, against his career; plus the moral issue of not immediately setting the Home Secretary's mind at rest. It was tough, the most difficult decision of his life. In the event he did his duty as he knew that General Sir Peter Inge would see it.

He got through to the Home Secretary in London and told him what had happened. But he also turned all his considerable persuasive powers on Parker-Reed. The man was so delighted by the news, so full of relief, that he agreed to go along with what Fernandez proposed.

The cloud cover had thickened, and it was gloomy, humid and threatening to rain when, at nine-fifteen the following morning, Stephen Parker-Reed left the 747 which had just touched down at Lisbon. He was carrying a second flight bag, similar to the first, with a brown-paper parcel inside.

The Home Secretary walked confidently through customs and went directly to the airport bar. He was feeling good for the first time in days; five hours' uninterrupted, happy sleep had taken years off him. He had no idea where he was to go from there, only that he should wait. He was sitting on a bar stool, sipping coffee and eating a doughnut when he was called, over the tannoy, to a telephone.

It was that women again, his tormentor. She told him to make his way immediately to the harbour in central Lisbon, at the mouth of the Tagus. There he was to make his way to the Lagoa boatyard and pick up a motor boat which would be waiting for him, hired in his name. In the boat there would be an envelope with further instructions.

The Home Secretary did not go directly to the harbour. He got through to the *Agincourt*, which was moored in the Tagus estuary, on the northern edge of Lisbon, and told Fernandez exactly what he was to do.

Meanwhile, in a small hotel down near Lisbon docks, Arsenio took over the telephone from his girlfriend and dialled the number of the *Miss Molly*. Shannon answered the call.

'Put Joe on the line,' said Arsenio.

'He's having a dip, so he is,' the Irishman told him.

Arsenio glanced out of the window. It was beginning to drizzle. 'Lovely morning for it,' he said. 'I was just checking that everything's OK.'

'Fine and dandy, boss.'

'I'll catch up with you later.'

Shannon put the receiver down with his two manacled hands. 'He'll kill me for this, so he will,' he told Shale.

'No great loss, mate,' said the sergeant.

The Lagoa boatyard was an unlovely establishment in an even less lovely area. It was almost beneath the enormous – more than two kilometres long – suspension bridge spanning the mouth of the Tagus and joining central Lisbon to the highway going south. The boat hired for Parker-Reed was small, its paintwork peeling, and it looked barely seaworthy. It had an outboard motor and was steered by means of a hand-held rudder. By now, as he stepped down into the boat, the Home Secretary was feeling less than happy about his mission. It was raining, and he had on a thin raincoat, but it was also hot and humid so that with one of his London suits on underneath it, he was sweating.

The boat rocked precariously, then settled down as he sat in it. Under the seat he found an envelope. Inside it was a simple, hand-printed message. 'Make slowly towards the statue,' he read. Statue. He looked around. There was only one statue. Across the other side of the river on a hilltop stood the Cristo-Rei, a twenty-eight-metre-high, smaller replica of the famous statue overlooking Rio de Janeiro. He pulled the string on the Mercury motor, surprised that it started first time. Then he was off, passing slowly under the suspension bridge, heavy traffic thundering seventy metres above him, a train rumbling beneath it on one of the underslung pair of railway lines.

Parker-Reed had an electronic tracking device in the top pocket of his jacket, but that was now of little further use to Fernandez. Watching from the dockside, Fernandez could plainly see the Home Secretary as the little boat cut a path through the sluggish waters of the river. There was no sense in him moving from where he was; he had men stationed in various strategic positions on both banks, each of them with receivers picking up the signals coming from Parker-Reed's tracker. The *Agincourt*, a kilometre distant, slowly closing in, was tracking the signals too, and she had the motor boat pinpointed in her telescope as large as life.

Tense with an excitement which made him forget about his nagging back, Fernandez wondered vaguely about the lovely-looking lady with coppery, glinting hair who cruised by him at the wheel of a Ford Fiesta, her bare forearm hanging out of the window and getting wet. She parked a couple of hundred metres from him at the dockside, near some steps going down into the water, on either side of which yachts were moored. She was only of passing interest to him; he forgot about her and fixed his attention back on the motor boat; it was getting smaller, but Parker-Reed was still clearly distinguishable.

The Home Secretary was most uncomfortable. The rain was seeping through the shoulders of his mackintosh, apart from which his body was damp with sweat. He was also feeling extremely insecure because there were many large craft moving around him – including one huge passenger liner heading in his direction and several of the Phoenician-style barges with big triangular sails which were typical of the area. No seaman, he was scared of being run down.

Suddenly, dead ahead of Parker-Reed's boat, the head and shoulders of a man in a black-rubber wetsuit and with a face mask with air tube attached popped out of the water. The diver lifted up his mask long enough to call out, 'Drop the bag over the side,' then he submerged.

Finally the Home Secretary knew why he had been told to wrap the money in plastic. He did as he was told and, relieved that his mission was more or less over, turned the boat around.

Arsenio grabbed the handles of the flight bag very firmly. Well below the surface, he began swimming back towards the dockside, where he had arranged that Kirsty would wait for him in the Fiesta.

Aboard the *Agincourt*, the watchers had seen very clearly what had occurred. The captain had her motors put on full speed ahead. Fernandez had seen the frogman appear, and the bag dropped, too, though not so clearly. His eyes searched the murky water. The man had to come up somewhere, then they'd have him.

Since they had tried to catch him before, in La Sagrada Familia, Arsenio was doubly wary. He felt confident that nobody could follow him now – except for just one way: a tracking device in the parcel. He had already got the parcel out of the bag and abandoned the bag while swimming. Now, as he reached the dockside and surfaced by a moored rowing boat, close to Kirsty, hanging on to the boat with one arm he sliced through the string of the parcel, put it on a wooden seat in the boat and unwrapped it. Should there be a tracker in the parcel, he would find it.

There was no such device beneath the brown paper – but there was no money either. Just bundles of plain white paper.

Fernandez had spotted him. The major was moving cautiously along the dockside towards the Fiesta, his hand on the butt of the Magnum inside his shirt, waiting for Arsenio to get out of the water before making his move. The girl, he realized, was an accomplice; she was still at the wheel of the car, watching Arsenio.

No money, just paper; then he had been tricked. They had rescued Carolyn – there was no other possibility. Arsenio's eyes fell on the man in the unzipped, thin waterproof jacket who was ambling towards Kirsty. He recognized him.

'Get the hell *out* of here, Kirsty,' he shouted,

then he was gone, down into the murky depths of the harbour.

Kirsty revved the engine, the wheels slipped on the greasy, wet concrete, and the car began to slither away. Fernandez took aim and shot out both back tyres. The girl brought the car to a skidding halt, leapt out and started to run, as the major was gabbling into his walkie-talkie. Another, armed commando appeared in front of her, pointing his gun.

'You're in a certain amount of trouble, young lady,' Fernandez told Kirsty as he snapped handcuffs on her.

'All trouble, that's me,' she responded with a wry little smile.

Fernandez's gaze swept over the broad expanse of river. They'd find him, they'd have to. The *Agincourt* was on the scene, making its way at full throttle into the area. There were men on every bank. They'd get him – either that or Fernandez would dedicate the rest of his life to tracking El Asesino down.

But they did not catch him. Arsenio got clean away.

OTHER TITLES IN SERIES FROM 22 BOOKS

Available now at newsagents and booksellers
or use the order form provided

continued overleaf . . .

All 22 Books are available at your bookshop, or can be ordered from:

22 Books
Mail Order Department
Little, Brown and Company
Brettenham House
Lancaster Place
London WC2E 7EN

Please enclose a cheque or postal order made payable to Little, Brown and Company (UK) for the amount due, allowing for postage and packing.

UK, BFPO & EIRE CUSTOMERS: Please allow 75p per item, to a maximum of £7.50.
OVERSEAS CUSTOMERS: Please allow £1 per item.

While every effort is made to keep prices low, it is sometimes necessary to increase cover prices at short notice. 22 Books reserves the right to show new retail prices on covers which may differ from those previously advertised in the books or elsewhere.

NAME ....

ADDRESS..

....

....

I enclose my remittance for £...............................